Secrets and Spies

Secrets and Spies

Tina Wells

with Stephanie Smith

Random House 🏠 New York

Text and illustrations copyright © 2023 by Tina Wells
Cover art and interior illustrations by Brittney Bond

All rights reserved. Published in the United States by Random House Children's Books, a division of Penguin Random House LLC, New York.

Random House and the colophon are registered trademarks of Penguin Random House LLC.

Visit us on the Web! rhcbooks.com

Educators and librarians, for a variety of teaching tools, visit us at RHTeachersLibrarians.com

Library of Congress Cataloging-in-Publication Data
Names: Wells, Tina, author. | Smith, Stephanie, author. | Bond, Brittney, illustrator.
Title: Secrets and spies / Tina Wells with Stephanie Smith; [illustrations by Brittney Bond].
Description: First edition. | New York: Random House Children's Books, [2023] | Series: Honest June; 3 | Audience: Ages 8–12. | Audience: Grades 4–6. | Summary: Eleven-year-old June must juggle friendship, first love, and the fallout from a newly discovered family secret involving the entire town—all while under a truth-telling spell.
Identifiers: LCCN 2022031161 (print) | LCCN 2022031162 (ebook) | ISBN 978-0-593-37894-6 (trade) | ISBN 978-0-593-37896-0 (ebook)
Subjects: CYAC: Honesty—Fiction. | Charms—Fiction. | Interpersonal relations—Fiction. | Families—Fiction. | Secrets—Fiction. | African Americans—Fiction. | Humorous stories. | LCGFT: Humorous fiction.
Classification: LCC PZ7.W46846 Sf 2023 (print) | LCC PZ7.W46846 (ebook) | DDC [Fic]—dc23

Printed in the United States of America
10 9 8 7 6 5 4 3 2 1
First Edition

For Mom & Dad

CHAPTER ONE

✦✦
✦

I sat in the office of the *Featherstone Post*, ready for our Monday editorial meeting, uncomfortably silent. Which, for me, was unusual. I loved writing for the school paper, and I was usually full of amazing, super-juicy story ideas. But no one wanted to hear what I was thinking. Because no one wanted to talk to me. They had good reason.

I had made a hot stinking mess of things for myself at school. After living a peaceful, friendly existence in Featherstone Creek for most of my eleven years, things took a turn and I managed to insult practically everyone at Featherstone Creek Middle School. Let me explain.

A few months earlier, at the Featherstone Creek Festival, I met a woman—er, fairy godmother—named Victoria.

She put me under a spell that forced me to tell the truth at all times. The truth about everything—my feelings, a friend's new haircut, whether or not I did my homework—*everything*. To *everyone*.

The spell, according to Victoria, was supposed to better my life. Help me live my real truth. Find inner peace or something like that. Instead, it made me stir up more drama than ever. I had a massive argument with my parents at a restaurant, where I yelled at the top of my lungs that I didn't want to go to Howard University—the college my dad went to—and be a lawyer just like him. I got put on punishment for several weeks. Then my friend Lee told me he wanted to hang out with my friend Nia. But I kinda maybe had a crush on him, and I didn't want my best friends to be boyfriend and girlfriend. So I didn't tell Nia how Lee felt, and Nia and I got into a huge fight when the truth eventually came out.

For my whole life I'd been used to keeping my thoughts to myself instead of telling people what I really thought, for fear of punishment or rejection or conflict. Victoria's pushing me to share my thoughts all the time wasn't easy for me. So I tried to get around her rules by starting a blog that would be a safe place for me to share my feelings when I thought the truth would be too much to handle. But it backfired.

I wrote down the good, the bad, the ugly, the petty,

and the downright mean stuff that I thought about every-one, especially during rehearsals for the recent school mu-sical, *The Wiz*. I wrote about my very confusing feelings for Lee, and how jealous I was about his feelings for Nia, and how I didn't want to tell Nia he liked her. I thought the blog was safe. I thought a password with numbers and letters would be enough to keep it secure. Until I found out my best friend hacked it and leaked my words to the world. Shoulda considered two-factor authentication.

Now the entire population of Featherstone Creek had canceled me.

Okay, *mayyyyyybe* I'd done something to deserve it. I did write a journal of truths I was too scared to say out loud, truths that were both nasty and nice (okay, mostly nasty). And, yes, I talked the most trash about Nia, my best friend who leaked the blog. The karma is not lost on me.

So I apologized. I wrote a column in the school newspaper explaining myself. And I'm still apologizing. I know I messed up big-time. I know people still think I'm dirt. And I know it's going to take time for people to forgive me.

But until they do, I try to make myself as unseen as pos-sible, sitting quietly in the back of the room, head down, quiet as a church mouse in our newspaper meeting.

I looked down at my notes, pretending to be busy but

really struggling to swallow the lump of loneliness in my throat. I wondered how long I would be left out in the cold.

Suddenly Quincy Aarons walked into the newsroom, talking quickly, his short dreadlocks bouncing with every word.

"I told you, I think it's true," he said animatedly to someone behind him. "I heard it the other day."

"You sure?" his friend asked.

"I'm positive. My father's cousin told me. And whatever he says is always true. He's picked the Super Bowl winners three years running. I trust him."

Quincy took a seat at one of the desks near the computers across from me, still talking with his hand flailing about whatever bit of gossip he thought was the biggest news of the day. Then Ms. West walked into the room. We all sat up and became quiet in her presence, ready to pitch stories. "Who's got something for me?" Ms. West said in greeting.

Quincy perked up. "I've got something. And it's big. Like, huge!"

Ms. West smiled at Quincy and took out a notebook. "Okay, let's hear it."

"A'ight," Quincy said, pausing for effect. "I heard from my father's cousin, who heard it from someone at the car wash. There's a big secret behind the people who founded Featherstone Creek. Nothing is what it seems."

"What does that even mean?" said Rachelle, raising one of her full eyebrows. "This isn't a story."

"Yes, it is!" Quincy said. "It's the biggest story we all should be reporting on right now! The truth behind Featherstone Creek. Don't you want to know? Everyone wants to know!"

"The truth is that Featherstone Creek was founded by freed slaves," said Jaron Williams, a seventh grader with braces and fair skin, freckles splashed across his cheeks. "Black people. This town was built and settled and continues to be built by Black people. For us, by us, fam."

"Not what I heard," Quincy said.

"What did you hear?" Ms. West said.

"That that's not all there is to the story."

"But you don't know what the actual story is?" Rachelle asked, resting her chin on her hand. Quincy stopped talking. Everyone looked at him, waiting for his answer. He stayed quiet.

"Then you don't have a story!" Rachelle fired back.

Quincy stammered, "I—I will soon."

The rest of the room joined in the chatter. But I sat back in my chair, silent. I was curious. Could there be a different story behind the founding of Featherstone Creek? My parents had told me the same story of the town's founding for as long as I could remember. That it was founded by freed slaves, some of them my ancestors. That my family was part of the town's long lineage of settlers and business owners. My mother is a third-generation doctor running a practice in Featherstone Creek, and my father founded his law firm here because he, too, wanted to be part of the tradition of Black entrepreneurs in this town.

Ms. West jumped in to keep the peace. "Everyone—your job as reporters is to go find out if there is a story. Quincy obviously has a lead on something, and he's chasing it. Maybe you all should do the same."

I nodded and digested Ms. West's words. Maybe there

was something to the rumor. And maybe I could crack the real story before Quincy did. At the least, maybe I could distract myself from my own drama by researching the drama behind the town's founding—and maybe other kids of Featherstone Creek would do the same. I could use the break, honestly.

We were a few weeks out from the annual spring camping trip to Lake Lanier, and there was no way I could see myself getting on a bus to go into the woods with people who truly thought I was the meanest of the mean girls.

Blake Williams, a new friend who had transferred to Featherstone Creek this fall, was more hopeful. She had visions of us bunking together in the woods and roasting marshmallows by the fire. "Seriously, no one's gonna remember this on the camping trip," she said on the phone. I'd called her for some math homework help when I got home from school that afternoon, and our conversation quickly turned to the upcoming trip.

"I cannot get on that bus," I repeated.

Blake had transferred here from Boston and had only lived in Featherstone Creek a few months. She didn't understand the deep roots I had here. No fewer than six generations of my family had lived here, built businesses here, delivered babies here, and supported this community. Which makes my saying in my "secret" blog a bunch of real-but-not-so-nice things about everyone in town, including the old man who runs the general store that's been here for over a hundred years, even more shocking.

"Listen, people make mistakes," Blake said. "You're eleven. Yeah, you said some nasty things in that blog. But you wrote an apology in the newspaper to make up for it. People can't hate you forever."

"They can try!" I said.

"I think you should go on the trip and do your best

to win everybody back," Blake said. "Just be extra nice to everyone. Go up to people, one-on-one, and explain yourself. Show them you really, truly mean your apology. If people can't accept it, then move on."

"Really, truly" sounded exactly like what Victoria had said I should do to get this spell lifted the last time I'd seen her. She said if I apologized to everyone I'd hurt with my blog and they forgave me, she'd finally remove the spell that was turning my life into a dumpster fire. I tried to imagine myself smiling at people as they threw daggers at my picture on a dartboard in the campground's lodge. I imagined myself staying strong as people laughed in my face when I told them I was sorry. I tried to block out the worst of all possibilities, including people using balled-up copies of my heartfelt column as kindling for a bonfire. I still didn't see my attendance at the school trip going well.

"Blake, really, how can anyone forget what I did?" I said. I certainly couldn't. I was pretty sure this would haunt me for the rest of my life!

"Seriously, people forget things. I'm sure by the time we get back from the trip, nobody will even remember or care. They'll be talking about something else."

I jumped up quickly, pacing around my room. "Then I have an idea—why don't you do something to distract people from what I did? Like start a food fight in the cafeteria, so everyone can be talking about something other than this stupid blog?"

Blake laughed. "No thanks, June. But you wait: this trip is probably the best thing for you. I gotta run—my mom's calling. Think about it."

After I hung up with Blake, my mind was already churning with worry about the trip. The idea of facing all my sixth-grade friends in the aftermath of the leak made me wince. But I thought about Victoria and what I needed to do to get rid of the spell. Under the truth-telling rules, I had to be honest with everyone about everything. But Victoria's latest requirement—to apologize face to face to those I had said hurtful things about in my blog—seemed like the hardest challenge yet. It meant I would see and feel people's reactions to my words in real time—no filters or screens or anything between us. A trip to the dentist sounded more pleasant.

But lifting the spell could also mean that things would be normal again. Or at least normal-ish. If Victoria ended it, I could live without someone watching over my shoulder. I could talk without fear of a sneeze attack, because Victoria would no longer spray fairy dust around when I attempted to lie (or even thought about lying). Because there would *be* no Victoria. And if I had learned anything from the last few months, there would be no lying, either.

So, like Blake said, maybe this trip would be the best thing for me.

Maybe.

✦

Instead of hanging out with my friends Olive and Nia and Lee, I spent most of my time after school alone, except for the days when I went to school newspaper meetings. Since I'd written my apology column, I hadn't been too excited to go to those. Field hockey season was over, and the school musical performances were finished for the year, but my former friend Nia was still playing basketball and Olive was busy with orchestra. Alvin, who was Lee's best friend and who had starred in our school's production of *The Wiz* with me, was tied up with STEM Club (yes, in addition to singing perfectly, going to church every week, and getting straight As). Lee was still avoiding me after the Nia/blog thing.

Since "the leak," I'd taken a break from posting my innermost thoughts online. But I missed having an outlet. I decided to go back to the old-fashioned way of storing personal secrets—I bought a good ol' diary with a lock on it, where I could write down my feelings about life. I resolved to keep it in a supersecret space underneath my mattress, and I hid the key behind a picture frame on my desk. After Nia's hack of my blog, I wasn't trusting online technology as a safe place to harbor my deep, dark secret truths. I couldn't say that a diary was any more secure, but it was all I had for now, especially because the upcoming trip would be technology-free . . . *if* I decided to go.

I reached for the brand-new pink journal, the spine still stiff and unbroken. I turned to a blank page and wrote some of my thoughts about what was going on in my life.

Dear Journal,

Here I am, alone in my room after school again. This isn't ever going to end, is it? There's no way people will ever forgive me! I wouldn't forgive me! I should leave Featherstone Creek. I can pack a bag and leave in the middle of the night, not disturbing my parents or anyone else, and keep walking down the main road, toward the highway. Maybe I could make it all the way to Savannah?

I sighed, tired of writing in the journal and longing for a distraction from my loneliness. I went to my desk and opened up my computer, letting my mind drift to another topic. I thought back to Quincy's chatter about the secret of Featherstone Creek. In all my eleven long years,

I'd never heard my parents talk about a secret or anything weird about the founding of the town.

"You know the real story of Featherstone Creek?"

What real story? What about Featherstone Creek? How would anything except the truth be known about the best town in all of Georgia, IMHO?

Suddenly I saw dust fall onto the top of my hand resting against my keyboard. I looked up. I knew exactly what—or rather, *who*—was about to make her presence known. The dust was always with me at this point, like that one character from the Peanuts cartoons who's always dirty. A plume of dust gathered into a small funnel; then the funnel reached down toward the floor, growing into a storm cloud. The shape of a woman appeared and fine-tuned into Victoria, all as I sat, nonplussed, at my desk. I didn't want to look her in the eye. I sighed and rolled my eyes.

"Well, hello to you, too, June," Victoria said, trying to get my attention. "You don't seem excited to see me, your dear friend."

I turned to her with an eyebrow raised. "You're my fairy godmother, not my dear friend."

"Right, well, but still, godmother, like *godly*, like *ethereal*," she said. "Anyway, you could at least sit up straight."

I turned and looked at her and shrugged. " 'Sup," I said.

"June, do you want me to help you out of your predicament, or are you going to keep disrespecting me?"

I finally sat up and looked directly at her eyes. I felt my throat in my chest, sitting heavy. Everything felt heavy these days. My clothes felt heavy. My hair, my thoughts.

"I did what you told me to do, and people still hate me," I blurted out. "I wrote the column in the newspaper to apologize to everyone and admit what I did was completely wrong, and look where it's gotten me. Nowhere."

Victoria dropped her head to one side. "It was never about going anywhere," Victoria said. "It was about expressing your truth, albeit in a respectful manner."

I sucked my teeth. "So, what now? You said that if I talked to people in person and gave them my heartfelt apology, you would lift the spell. Now, do you promise, with all your might, that if I apologize to everyone on the camping trip, you will lift the spell?"

Victoria looked at me and adjusted her crown. I was tired. I needed relief. And Victoria knew it. She gave one nod.

"Nothing but the truth," she said. "The whole weekend in the woods."

"I solemnly swear to tell the whole truth and nothing but the truth, on my favorite pair of shoes and a bowl of Lucky Charms!" I yelled.

Victoria crossed her arms. She stood there motionless, her eyes looking me up and down. I didn't move. A strand of hair fell in my eyes, and I was too intent on finding a way to get out of this spell that I let it block my left pupil until Victoria gave me a confirmation.

"Nothing but the truth," she said. "And I'll lift the spell."

And with that, Victoria stood back and started to spin in a tight circle in the middle of my room, the dust giving way to a tornado until I couldn't see her anymore. I let out an exasperated breath. I was going to have to go on that camping trip. I was going to have to apologize to everyone face to face. And no matter what, I was going to get this spell lifted once and for all.

I finally moved the hair out of my eye and got up to look in the closet for my sleeping bag.

CHAPTER TWO

✦ ✦
✦

"Girl, you still alive?"

"Very funny, Chloe," I said, rolling my eyes. Chloe Lawrence-Johnson was one of my closest friends. Though she lived across, like, twenty states, in California, she was the person I called when I needed to talk to someone who understood me completely but who didn't live any-where near Featherstone Creek. Sometimes I needed an outsider's point of view. At other times I just didn't trust anyone in Featherstone Creek with the information. And now, Tuesday after school, alone in my room, I needed Chloe more than ever, especially since no one in this town would talk to me.

"Juuuuuuune!" Chloe said over the phone, shaking me out of my funk. "Seriously, though, you good?"

I looked at myself in the mirror, and my eye caught the large backpack in my closet, ready to be filled with clothes for the camping trip. I dreaded the thought. I knew that going on this trip would be the final step in getting Victoria's spell lifted, but it was going to be torturous.

"How in the world can I be good?" I asked. "I feel like everywhere I turn, people are giving me side-eye."

"For your burn book?" Chloe said.

"Can we not call it that?" I begged. "It was supposed to be a private journal."

"Where you talked trash about everyone," Chloe said.

"Where I had to put my private truths so I didn't lie in real life! So I wouldn't be embarrassed. And so I wouldn't betray Victoria and get attacked by fairy dust for lying to people!"

"Girl, don't explain your way out of it," Chloe said, her voice rising to the pitch of a robin's. "Own up to it."

"I did!" I said, waving my arm for effect, even though Chloe couldn't see it. "I wrote the column in the paper!"

"Well then, chill out. You going on the school trip?"

"I dunno," I said. I felt a rock drop in my stomach. Every time someone mentioned that trip, I felt nauseous. I knew I had to go to get the spell lifted, but I dreaded being in the company of everyone I'd insulted.

"Is Nia going?"

"Probably," I said. "I don't know."

Chloe sounded like she was sucking on a lollipop. She smacked her lips. "What are you going to do about Nia?"

I scrunched up my face. It was Nia's fault I was in this pickle. She'd taken my private journal, stolen the password (okay, she'd figured out the password because, in all honesty, anyone who'd known me for longer than fifteen minutes could have figured out what it was—middle name plus my year of birth), and made the journal public. "I don't know. I'm still mad at her. Because of her I'm the town troll."

"No, girl, because of your own words you're the town troll," Chloe reminded me. She was not wrong. I sighed again. "Just keeping it real!" she said.

"Thank you for your realness," I said cynically. "A few people have come up to me and thanked me for my honesty. Like, Ms. West said it was brave to write the apology. But the crew is keeping it chilly. Well . . . except for Alvin. He's been really cool. Maybe because I didn't say that many mean things about him in the blog."

There was another possible reason. Alvin and I had started becoming closer friends after we did *The Wiz* together—he'd played the Scarecrow, and I'd starred as Dorothy. He was funny, talented, and nice. And it was possible by then that I might have liked him more than I used to like Lee, I thought. I didn't think I'd said anything bad about him in the blog. . . .

"You called him a computer nerd with a fade in need of a trim," Chloe reminded me.

Ugh, did I? Must have been in the earlier posts, before we started hanging out. I gritted my teeth tightly. "But I also called him super talented and cool."

"Doesn't mean he forgot about the nerd part."

I wanted to forget about the nerd part. I wanted to forget about all the parts. "Anyway, Victoria said the only way she'd lift the spell is if I went on the camping trip and apologized to everyone in person."

"Wow," Chloe said. "Okay, get packing, then."

"I am!"

"Good!"

"Good!"

We hung up. I was about to put my cell phone down but immediately heard a ping. Speak of the devil, it was Alvin.

ALVIN: Wanna ride to the creek?

My heart did a flip. Of course Alvin was more than a computer nerd. (Why had I even *written* that? *Cringe!*) He was a great singer and actor and a great guy. We talked a lot in classes, about school assignments, music, movies, and video skits on YouTube. He told me funny stories from church, and I told him about whatever funny things I noticed at home and at school. I didn't know Alvin was so hilarious until we started hanging out during the musical, and honestly, I liked every new thing I got to know about him.

Before the musical, Alvin had been best friends with Lee. But now I was certain Lee hated me. This is how the real friend drama had started: Lee had asked me to ask Nia to hang out sometime, and I didn't want to because I didn't want to share Lee with Nia. Lee was one of my oldest friends. We'd grown up just down the block from each other, and both our families had summer houses on Lake Lanier. I'd always felt some type of way about Lee, and still kinda did, but you know how these things go. (Well, okay, maybe *I* don't, but everyone else does!) Anyway, Nia told me one day she was interested in Lee, too, but I didn't tell Nia that Lee was interested in her. I kept a secret from him and kept him from hanging out with Nia because I didn't want him to have feelings for her— because *I* had feelings for him.

Of course, they both found out later that I'd withheld the truth from them. And I'd been a horrible friend for trying to keep them apart. I know. It was bad—selfish. I wanted to fix it, but Lee still hadn't said anything to me about it. He'd barely said *anything* to me at all. My parents invited his family over for dinner last weekend and he came, but he didn't say much. I mean, he was polite. Like, he asked me to pass the dinner rolls and whether I'd finished my math homework. But besides that, he paid more attention to his video game console than to me. And that wasn't like him. It wasn't cool. It was *cold*. I knew he was still mad about how everything had gone down. Maybe *he*'d canceled me, too?

Before the drama, Lee and I always went to the creek together. Now he was probably going to the creek, and anywhere else, with Nia.

Losing two best friends in one go really hurt. And I deserved it—even if the punishment was that I was alone most of the time because no one besides Alvin wanted to hang out with me. Somehow, through all of this, Alvin was still a friend. Of course I'd go to the creek with him.

JUNE: Hi! Meet u outside in 20

✦

Alvin was wearing an oversized bomber jacket and high-top sneakers as he biked toward my house. I stood in my driveway, my bike in between my legs, watching anxiously as he pedaled toward me. I was excited to see him, a real

friend. A good-looking, talented, real friend. I said hello eagerly, maybe too eagerly, as he approached.

"Hi," he said quickly. "I have to collect some river water for a science assignment. Thought since I bike by your house on the way, I'd ask you to join, and maybe you'd want to come."

I felt my cheeks getting warm. I was surprised he wanted to spend time with me, the school blabbermouth. I mean, we talked at school, but this was our first time hanging out one-on-one outside of a classroom or the cafeteria. Maybe he hadn't read the blog? *Everyone* had read the blog. But I couldn't dwell on that. I'd have to take whatever friendship I could get and be grateful for it now. I accepted the invitation before he could take it back. "Cool! Let's go."

I followed him to the park. The trees had buds, but flowers hadn't yet bloomed on most of them. We rolled past a few moms with their strollers full of small kids bundled in sweaters. We crossed into the park, and Alvin beelined for the river. I followed him, making a left in front of the ice cream truck that I used to go to with Lee.

"Just need a few vials here," Alvin said. He hopped off his bike and let it fall over onto the riverbank.

He smiled and pulled a few small bottles out of his backpack. I watched as he carefully scooped up the river water, capped two of the vials, and placed them into a small container to keep them upright. He looked at me. "You don't have Mrs. Lewis for science?"

"No, I have Mr. Duncan. We're not doing that project yet, I guess."

"Right," he said. Then he looked away. He was hard to read today. I tried to figure out what he thought of me. Had he read the blog but didn't care what I'd written? I wanted to ask. *I should ask. I'll—*

"You going on the camping trip?" he asked.

I froze. "Um, maybe. Are you?"

"Yeah, of course. Everybody's going. Why wouldn't you go?"

Maybe he hadn't realized that the entire sixth grade had tried to erase me from their minds. "I'm not exactly the most popular kid at school right now."

"What do you mean?" he asked. "Because of that blog?"

So he *did* know. My heart sank. "Yeah."

He went back to collecting river water and filling up a vial. "Yeah, but you apologized in your column. It's over."

"Not in most people's eyes," I said.

He placed the capped vial with the others in the plastic container, then carefully put the entire container in his backpack. "I'm done. I mean, with the assignment. You should go on the trip. No one's tripping over that blog anymore."

I wanted him to be right. What if he *was* right? Obviously, people had hated me at first, but what if I'd gotten too in my head about it? Maybe everybody had moved on but I still thought they hated me. What if everyone was like "whatever," and I didn't have to apologize to win them back? Would my apology even count? Would Victoria remove the spell?

"Besides," Alvin said, before mounting his bike and pushing off. "I feel like you know more about Lake Lanier than anyone else does. Maybe more than Lee. Just think— we'd all have more fun if you were there."

He cruised down the path away from the creek and toward the main exit. I pedaled behind him, smiling, hoping he was right. If not, I hoped he meant at least *he* would have fun with me there.

✦

I got home and put my bike away, still thinking about Alvin. I wondered if I would have a good time on the camping trip if I just hung out with him the entire time. Would he save me if somebody tried to put fire ants in my sleeping bag? Or ran off with my clothes while I showered?

As I walked through the kitchen to grab a glass of milk and a snack before I went to my room, I thought about Alvin some more—especially what he'd said about having more fun if I was there.

I opened the refrigerator door and pushed aside the orange juice, looking for the almond milk—but then I felt a gust of air. It drifted out from inside the refrigerator, like vapor from dry ice. It got thicker and thicker as it swirled around me and then coasted toward the kitchen counter, where it settled and formed a figure sitting in front of me. The details of the form took shape—long hair, sparkly dress, magic wand in hand. Victoria.

"June, June, June," she said. "Hungry?"

I sighed and turned back to the refrigerator. "A little."

I grabbed an apple and a bottle of water and shut the door. Victoria's eyes never looked away from mine.

"I saw that dear Alvin also craved your attention," she said, crossing her arms.

"What do you mean?" I said. "He asked to hang out, so I did. No one else is asking me to hang out these days."

"Of course, doll, but that's not what I'm talking about. I think Mr. Alvin fancies you."

"*Fancies* me?" I said. "We went to the creek. What's fancy about that?"

Victoria giggled and uncrossed her arms. "That's not what I mean, June. I think he might like you. Like in the way that you like Lee. But either way, he's been quite caring toward you, even in the roughest of times. Might be worth spending more time with him."

"Yeah, he's cool," I said. And smart. And talented. And kind of cute. *June! Focus—don't let this become another crush. You saw what a mess you made of the Lee thing.*

"Just cool?" Victoria said. "Remember, the truth will set you free."

I took a bite of the apple. "The truth has done anything but set me free."

"Okay, maybe you've had your struggles, but still! I remember what you wrote about Alvin in your journal. Don't forget: you owe him an apology, too. He might be more sweet on you than you realize."

I shrugged my shoulders and tried to brush off what she was implying—that Lee's best friend had a crush on me after all that had happened. I didn't want to think about messing up another friendship when it was just starting. I didn't want to feel rejected, like I did with Lee. Maybe the less I spoke with Alvin, the less likely that either of these things would happen.

"Anyway," Victoria said, "are you excited about the camping trip??"

"No," I said. "Do I *have* to go on the trip?"

"Do you want me to lift the spell?"

I sighed. I knew there was no other way to get this unfortunate truth-telling spell removed. I looked up at the ceiling, then at Victoria. My shoulders slumped.

"Don't forget to pack a flashlight," Victoria said. She stood up from the counter and began spinning slowly, then faster, until she was swept up in a cloud of dust that disappeared into thin air. I took an angry bite of my apple, grabbed my water bottle, and slunk upstairs to my room to hide.

Dear Journal,

Could Alvin be the new Lee? As in, Lee was my go-to hang-out guy. My best guy friend, the one I went to the creek with and rode bikes with and smiled with until my eyes got all squinty every time we were together. But now Alvin is around. Alvin texts me to hang out. Alvin thinks I should go camping. He says no one's tripping about the blog. He thinks we'd all have more fun with me there! Is he right? I know one thing—getting to spend more time with Alvin would be the best reason to go on this camping trip, aside from getting this spell lifted by apologizing to everyone there.

CHAPTER THREE

✦

The annual school trip to Lake Lanier was a big deal. Every year the entire sixth grade went to a campsite at the lake to spend an extended weekend in the woods. There would be roasting marshmallows and sharing scary stories around the campfire, but teachers also organized activities and games to get us to work in teams. We were supposed to learn about nature, as well as how to be helpful and kind to one another.

I'd been looking forward to the trip ever since I heard about it during the first weeks of school. My family spent many weekends and vacations at our country house in Lake Lanier. I knew how to get around the lake. As did Lee—we explored Lake Lanier's woods and trails together all the time. That is, we did when we were friends.

But now we weren't friends anymore. At the least, we weren't *friendly.*

Now the idea of being in the middle of the woods with the entire sixth grade, who thought I was the uncoolest of the uncool, was nerve-racking. I thought about what would happen if I were left alone with Carmen Becker, who I'd said was afraid of her own shadow. Would she take revenge on me? Put a poisonous spider in my suitcase?

I dreaded being alone. I also dreaded being left out. Not going meant this doggone spell would never be lifted. And I wouldn't get a chance to smooth things over with my friends. If I wanted to kill the spell by apologizing to everybody personally, I had to go camping. So, a-camping we would go.

Wednesday night at school was the parents' meeting—each year a handful of parents volunteered to help plan the activities for the kids. My mom couldn't go on the campout—she'd be on call that weekend—but she wanted to hear all the details anyway. I was going along so I could also get the scoop on the trip and perhaps beg the chaperones to place me in a cabin by myself (or maybe with Blake) and perhaps provide twenty-four-hour surveillance so that no one could kidnap me in the middle of the night. I didn't think that was too much to ask, given the circumstances.

We took seats in the middle of the auditorium, a few rows from the stage. I fiddled with my braids—even though I was hesitant about going on the trip, I'd gotten braids just in case. They'd be an easy 'do while in the woods. I looked around for familiar faces, and as I turned to the right, I saw a not-so-friendly one: Nia's. She was with her mother. I cringed.

My mom waved politely at them, but I pretended I hadn't seen Nia. I looked down at my lap, then over to the left. My mom called over my head to Mrs. Shorter: "Hey, how you doing?" Then, to me, "June, you see Nia over there?"

I didn't want to see her. I glanced up for a hot second, hoping she wouldn't look my way. Instead, Nia chose that exact moment to gaze in my direction with her big almond-shaped eyes. Then we glared at each other for what seemed like a day and a half (but was actually more like two seconds). Finally, we each gave a single nod and went back to looking at our laps. I rolled my eyes while no one could see me.

When Blake walked into the auditorium with her mom, she gave me a big smile and wave. "Hey, girl!" I said, loud enough for Nia to hear me. Nia had this weird grudge against Blake, and I had no idea why. I knew it would annoy Nia that I just gave Blake and her mom the biggest hello ever.

A few minutes later, Olive Banks—the best friend who was still speaking to me—walked into the auditorium with her mother. Olive looked happy, a wide smile on her round face, her short curly hair bouncing as she walked. It wasn't like Olive wasn't mad at me. She was still pretty peeved I had called her a pushover on my blog. But she was very chill; she rarely stayed angry for long, and she wanted everyone to get along whenever possible. She was a peacemaker. She should really work for the United Nations. That's what I should have written in that dumb blog.

Olive gave me a small hug and then walked past me toward Nia. Olive sat down in the row in front of her, and the two of them started chatting as if they weren't sitting in the same dang auditorium as their (former) best friend. *Okay, y'all really going to be like that? Fine.*

Then Lee walked in. I mean, of course he was going to be here because this event was all about the lake. That was his playground. His happy place. I watched as Lee walked down the auditorium aisle with his grandmother. I tried to catch his eye as he lumbered by, but he never looked up. Instead, he crossed the space toward the opposite end of the seats and sat in front of Olive and Nia. Sigh. . . . Looked like Lee was getting more time with Nia after all, just like he'd wanted.

I propped my elbow on my knee and plopped my head into my hand. If this assembly was any indication of

how the camping trip would go, then it looked like I'd be spending most of my time alone.

Finally, Alvin walked into the auditorium in front of his mother, who stopped to say a quick hello to one of his teachers. Alvin looked up at me with his wide brown eyes. We locked eyes. He gave a nod, tossing his natural curls back, and walked toward me.

He was in front of me before I could look away. "Hey, June. Hi, Dr. Jackson," he said.

"Hi, Alvin," my mom said warmly.

I didn't say anything. I smiled. I think I was blushing. Why was I blushing? "Hi," I said. I finally exhaled a bit.

The school bell rang, signaling the start of the meeting. Ms. West took the microphone at the front of the stage. "Good evening, everyone. Thank you so much for coming. Tonight is the start of planning for our upcoming camping trip for grade six. Who's excited?"

The room exploded with cheers and clapping—minus me.

Each of the sixth-grade teachers came forward to talk about their role on the trip and what activities they would run. Hiking. Kayaking. Planting trees with the parks commission. They also talked about the things we'd been doing in school ahead of the trip. "Our sixth graders have really come together as a group this year, supporting one another. They've collaborated on a number of projects to upgrade our school grounds, and they've done some volunteer work, like with our Creeks club," Ms. West said. "And we just finished our school musical, in which a number of sixth graders gave great performances."

I looked down at my feet. My stomach grumbled, and I felt my skin get hot. I could feel the mean stares coming toward me from everyone in the room. The auditorium became super quiet. I could hear my pulse in my ears. Why did she have to mention the school musical? Why remind people of my horrible secret blog, the blog that had been released the weekend of the musical?

I looked out from under my right armpit toward where Nia was sitting. I closed my eyes because I didn't want to know if she was looking my way. But I finally cracked one eye open. Sure enough, she was looking toward me with a smirk on her face. I covered my head with my hands and hoped Ms. West would change the subject soon.

After the meeting, my mom took me to our favorite restaurant, the Crab Shack. Dad would meet us there after he left the office. I hadn't been to the Crab Shack since the day when I yelled at the top of my lungs that I wasn't going to Howard and I couldn't take the pressure of being eleven years old in this family anymore. I had made such a scene that Dad got up from our table and sat by the bar. I could have gotten an Oscar for my performance that night. But now we were back, and we both prayed that none of the same waitstaff were working tonight.

A hostess walked us to a booth toward the back. Not one staffer even gave us a second look as we cruised by. Maybe kids threw hissy fits there all the time!

The hostess handed us menus and left to get us glasses of water. I kept my head low, not wanting anyone to recognize me. I buried my head in the multipage menu— they still had that cheese dip I liked. Dad popped in and said his hellos and got settled. After a few minutes, a server came to the table. "Hi, I'm Sheila, and I'll be serving you tonight," she said. "What can I get you all to drink?"

I recognized the voice immediately. Sounded like Victoria.

"Hi there," Mom said in her usual polite tone.

Sheila? I thought. I glared at her face as she stood there grinning at my dad while he ordered three iced teas for us. I gritted my teeth. Definitely Victoria, acting like a waitress named Sheila. It was so frustrating that Victoria could literally turn into whoever she wanted. She most loved to show up when I least expected her to, around people I least wanted her to interact with. The last time we were here, Victoria had shape-shifted into our server. It seemed she had gotten herself a permanent gig. I hoped she was making some good tips.

Sheila went to get our drinks, then returned with the iced teas. "What can I get for you?" she prompted again.

My father glanced at the menu and announced his order. "I'll have the grilled chicken sandwich," he said, looking Victoria straight in the face.

"And I'll have the Cobb salad. June, you want the wings? And the dip?"

I nodded and avoided eye contact.

"That waitress looks familiar," Mom said after she'd turned and left. "I think we had her last time. She was nice." I took a huge gulp of my iced tea. *If you only knew the mayhem that lady has put me through,* I thought.

"June, how are you feeling about the camping trip?" Dad asked.

"F-fine," I said, deciding to keep my answers brief and quiet. The truth is, I was ready for the trip like I was ready to go to the dentist to have a cavity filled—it needed to be done, but it wasn't going to be fun, especially if none of my friends would speak to me. I didn't want to reveal too much, so maybe the less I said, the less my parents would ask about it. "Just gonna pack light, I guess," I said. I felt a slight itch in my nose, the telltale sign that Victoria was warning me not to lie. I reached for my napkin to rub my nose lightly, and to shield my face in case I had a sneezing attack.

Ten minutes later, "Sheila" came back to drop off the food, winking at me as she put the plate of wings in front of me. She kept cool and quickly went away after holding my gaze for just a second. It was Victoria, right? Hard to tell without the tiara and puffy gown. But she had reminded me multiple times she was listening to my every word. Maybe she thought I needed to have an important conversation with my parents tonight. . . .

Mom jumped into the conversation. "Speaking of school, I haven't heard much about the school paper. How's the writing coming along?"

I perked up. "It's good!" I said between bites of chicken. "I think I'm going to start working on a big new story."

Okay, I actually had no idea how big that "truth" about Featherstone Creek was going to be. But it was big enough that everyone at the paper was digging into it, and I wanted to be the first to figure it out. "I heard there's apparently some hidden secret about Featherstone Creek."

Dad looked at Mom quickly but kept eating his sandwich and sneaking looks at the football game on the television above the bar. Mom stuffed her mouth with Cobb salad and looked down. She gave one nod. There was an awkward silence. She suddenly didn't seem interested in my work on the paper, even though she was the one who'd asked about it. She was the one who'd supported my decision to stay on the paper when Dad was trying to encourage me to do the debate club instead. I was surprised she wasn't cheering me on.

Mom quickly changed the subject. "Any other drama or arts stuff going on? You seemed to want to pursue acting. Have they announced more plays or performances at school?"

I followed Mom's train of thought. "Not yet," I said, "but we should start looking into representation. And I might have to pursue the arts outside of Featherstone

Creek if there are no real opportunities for me here. Like, maybe I should start auditioning for commercials?"

"Let's see if we can make it through the next term with good grades, and then we can talk about additional extracurriculars," Dad said.

I forgot about the camping trip for the rest of dinner, more concerned instead with the barbecue sauce–drenched wings on my plate (and now in my belly).

When we finished, my parents paid the check and got up from the table. As I scooted across the booth's leather seat, I took a closer look at the bill for signs of fairy godmother. I opened the check holder to verify—and a waft of fairy dust flew in my face. My nose instantly became irritated, and I almost sneezed all over the table "Sheila" had just wiped clean.

I knew it.

Sheila *was* Victoria! Just like I'd suspected. That woman was going to have to try thinking of new tricks, because I was pretty sure I had all of her usual ones figured out already.

I quickly closed the check, got up, and walked out behind my parents, trying to hold my sneeze in as I left.

Mom and Dad were

unusually quiet in the car. They turned on the radio to listen to a podcast interview with some professor. Maybe they were truly interested, but I was so bored by the conversation that I fell asleep. Once we pulled into our garage, I shook myself awake and shuffled into the house. Mom and Dad then quickly went to their respective offices, claiming they had work to do. I went up to my bedroom and started to get ready for bed.

Before I got into my nighttime routine, though, I reached for my journal. The gears in my mind were in overdrive, thinking about what had been said and *not* said over dinner.

Dear Journal,

Was it me, or were my mom and dad super weird after I told them about the rumored secret of Featherstone Creek? Do they know something? Are they involved somehow? I mean, Dad was way more into his sandwich than the story. (Or was he just annoyed—again—that I'm not on the debate team?) Mom was, like, bothered. Have they heard this before? Did they talk to Quincy's father's cousin from the car wash? I don't know. But now I'm even more curious to find out the real secret.

CHAPTER FOUR

Thursday morning I dragged myself out of bed. Before the blog leak, I used to race to school excitedly, eager to see people, go to class, take notes, talk with friends. Now I dreaded the thought of school. I just didn't know what to expect anymore—would anyone talk to me? Would I get dirty looks or sad stares, or would I just flat-out be ignored?

I'd just picked up my books at my locker and was slogging through the crowded hallway when I heard a familiar laugh behind me. I turned around. Nia was walking toward me. I did a double take—surely she wasn't coming over to chat with me. Right?

Her smile drooped as she saw me in front of her. I turned away and continued walking toward the homeroom door.

But before I could squeeze through, she was beside me. "Hey," she said.

Was I being punked? Was this Nia's big confrontation with me, in front of the entire school in the hallway before homeroom, where everyone would watch and then gossip about what happened before first period? Were we supposed to talk . . . or fight? I expected more anger from her, but she was super chill. *Should I be angry?* I looked around. Kids were hustling to their classes like normal, books in hand, laughing and talking. No one was really paying attention to us.

"How's it going?" she asked shyly. *How's it going?* I thought. *Oh, you know, just trying to pick up the shattered pieces of my life and put them back together, thanks to you.* This couldn't be happening. But it was, and Nia was trying to be as normal as possible, maybe expecting me to raise my voice and act out. But instead, I played cool, too. "It's all good," I said coolly. "You?"

"You know, same old," she said. She fell into pace with me as we entered the classroom and walked toward our seats. "How's stuff with the paper?"

Was she really asking about my life right now? As if she really cared? As if I really wanted to tell her anything about myself after what had happened? I mean, she'd already revealed my innermost thoughts to the entire world; why on earth would I trust her with any info about me? I resolved to give her answers that seemed safe.

"It's going," I said.

"Cool," she said, and gave a half smile.

Something felt off. Why was she being nice to me? Were we ever going to discuss what had happened? Were we ever going to have a drag-out fight about it?

Nia quickly sat down and tossed her long wavy hair over her shoulder. I shook my head and shrugged off my confusion. My forehead unscrunched. I took a breath and then slid into my seat in the row next to Nia's. I wasn't sure if we were friends again or if all was forgiven about the blog. But I did know that talking felt better than not talking. I took out my books for class, smiled to myself, and hoped this was the beginning of a truce between Nia and me.

The entire sixth grade was antsy during lunch. Everyone was tethered to their email, waiting for the camping trip group assignments to come in. An email with a single letter, *A* through *L*, should have been sent to each student by lunchtime, and all the kids were waiting anxiously to see who they would be grouped with for the trip.

There were 120 students in the sixth grade, and we were going to be divided into twelve cohorts of ten students. The groups would be mixed, but the sleeping cabins would be separated by gender. Each group would have an RA—a residential advisor—who usually was a parent or teacher chaperone. The groups would eat together, do chores together, take workshops together, travel to camp together. This was going to be intense.

I was sitting at my usual table with the crew; I felt a bit

more comfortable joining everyone after Nia's greeting this morning. Right on time, every sixth grader's tablet lit up with their assignment email.

> **To: June Jackson**
> **From: Ms. West**
> **Subject: FCMS Spring Break Camping Trip**
> **Group Assignments**
>
> **Dear June,**
> **You have been assigned to group K.**

"K!" Alvin and I yelled at the same time. We looked at each other. I smiled. At least I would be with someone who enjoyed my company right now! Someone who would lend a helping hand if I fell into a creek or would share a bag of trail mix if I was hungry during a hike. We gave each other a fist bump.

"B!" Olive and Blake exclaimed, breaking my train of thought. They gave each other a high five. Then the girls looked at Nia.

"D?" Nia and Lee said, confused. They looked as if they hadn't expected to be grouped together. They'd been hanging out as friends for weeks. Wasn't this what Lee wanted? Nia didn't look so sure. Either way, I didn't want to dwell on the negative.

"Well, at least we all have a buddy within our group!" I said excitedly.

Everyone fell into conversation about the trip—who would bring what supplies, what food they thought would be available, who should bring additional snacks. Nia and Lee nervously chatted with each other. Lee talked quickly, excited to tell Nia about his new camping gear and knowledge of the woods. Nia looked more hesitant—nonplussed, even. Wasn't she excited to be in a group with Lee? Was she just playing it cool in front of him?

Alvin looked over at me. "So should I bring the marshmallows and graham crackers for s'mores, or you got it?"

"Those are camping staples! The school will bring them," I said. "You ever been camping before?"

"A few times with Lee," Alvin said. "Mostly in his backyard, though."

"You don't even own a sleeping bag, do you, Alvin?" Lee laughed. "You always borrow one of mine."

"I got one a few weeks ago," Alvin said. He turned back to me. "Have you been camping before?

"Maybe once?" I replied. "Also maybe in Lee's backyard. Not the same as being in the wild woods."

"Ah, we'll be fine," Lee said. "If a bear comes along, I'll scare him off for both of you."

I felt a little tickle in my chest. Lee didn't seem to be

ignoring me after all. In fact, he'd just made a joke about protecting me. That was better than pretending I didn't exist! I'd take it! I laughed between bites of my sandwich and shared my chips with Olive. Nia wondered out loud if she should get her braids redone before the trip.

"If you go to the salon, I'll go with you," I said. "Maybe I'll get my braids redone, too."

"I'll let you know," she said, smiling.

My heart fluttered. It felt nice to be back in the good graces of my friends. I didn't know if they'd all forgiven me, but at least they were being polite. Maybe my Lake Lanier Apology Tour would be better received than I thought. If my closest friends could let me back into the fold, maybe the rest of the class would soon follow.

I felt a gust of wind tickle my nose—not fairy dust, but a gentle breeze that wafted around my face. I thought of Victoria. Maybe she was sending a signal of hope? I said a silent thank-you as I finished my lunch and continued to swap notes about the camping trip with the gang.

CHAPTER FIVE

✦ ✦
✦

I was one of the first people in the newspaper office for the meeting after school on Thursday. I sat down at a computer near where Ms. West usually sat. I couldn't wait to start digging into the Featherstone Creek mystery. I was determined to be the first to report on it—especially since Mom's brush-off after asking about the school paper at the Crab Shack. Maybe my story would get the front page again. . . . I really needed another win! I started gathering my notes and googling articles and documents about Featherstone Creek, some of which went back to the 1800s.

Featherstone Creek had been founded by former slaves and incorporated by other free Black people who started businesses, founded schools and a hospital, built

Featherstone Creek early days

search

roads and houses, and passed down their investments and property to future generations. The town was proud of its roots. In recent generations, its population had become more diverse. People of all colors flocked here because they appreciated and honored the town's history.

I was so lost in my Google search, I didn't notice that the rest of the students had arrived for the meeting until Ms. West spoke up. "Okay, everyone, what's going on for the next issue? Who wants to start pitching?"

My hand shot up. "What about that story about the founding of Featherstone Creek? The rumors about some big secret about how the town was founded. Quincy, you hear back from your uncle or cousin or whoever?"

"Nope," he said.

This was an opportunity. I bet I could solve this mystery. My mom would know tons of people I could talk to. "I want to find out what it is."

"Yeah, you and everyone else," Tasha Simms blurted out. She pushed her pink glasses further up on her nose. "I've heard the same rumors. Lots of people have been trying to crack that story for years and haven't done it."

"Why not?" I asked. "Maybe they didn't do enough digging. You know, maybe they didn't check facts, talk to sources, research documents. . . ."

"I remember George Murtaugh in eighth grade worked all year to crack that story, but he still couldn't do it. He graduated from middle school and still didn't get to write anything about it."

"That's true, I remember," Ms. West said. "Just for your background, kids, for years there have been whispers about the founding of Featherstone Creek. Whenever magazines or newspapers want to shine a light on us, the older members of the community shut it down. They offer lots of 'no comments,' or sometimes the story just mysteriously falls apart. It seems the descendants of the founding families take the same stance on media that their ancestors did. There are even whispers that the most senior members of the seven founding families still meet to discuss how to keep secrets secret."

Ms. West looked at me. My family—my mother's

mother's mother's mother's mother's *mother*—was part of one of the founding families, and the reason why we've stayed here ever since. I had never heard about any meetings among my family members to discuss town business. But there was one thing my mom did that she always brushed aside questions about—she had a mysterious book club meeting on one Thursday night each month. But I never saw my mom reading anything besides medical journals or patient files. Was that weird? Maybe she listened to audiobooks on her commute to work? IDK. Worth asking.

"Well, I've been looking into the rumor, too," I said. "But I feel like I've heard the same thing Quincy has. All talk, no real proof."

"See? Maybe it's a waste of time," Tasha said.

"I don't think it's a waste of time at all," Ms. West said. "Pursuing something that speaks to you is never a waste of time."

"Well, I want to do it," I said.

"Me too," Tasha said. I hadn't planned on so much competition for a scoop. What would happen if someone else got to the truth first, before me?

"I betcha I get the story before both of you," Quincy said.

Ms. West interrupted the building excitement. "It's great if a few of you want to pursue the story at once.

I think you all should look into it. You should explore whatever leads you have or rumors you've heard. Do your historical research. And maybe you all work together on this one and work as a team. The biggest scoops in news history often came from a group of reporters coming together, not just one person."

My mind processed the idea of sharing a scoop. Two or three reporters digging into a story are probably better than one. And my name could be on the front page of the paper, just not alone.

But what if someone found out something bad about Featherstone Creek? About the original founders? About my own family? I'd never heard anyone say anything about my elders, and I know we have great family history here. But this secret—what if it, like, changed everything? And what if I found out some bad stuff about my own family? What would I do?

"Sound like a plan, guys?" Ms. West asked. "We'll have a few of you digging into the Featherstone Creek story, and you can update us on what you've found until we're ready to file something. Take your time. Be thorough. Be truthful. Know your history. And ask me for any advice or help you need."

I turned my attention back to my notes while other kids continued pitching stories. I gritted my teeth. Competition made me more driven to find out the truth about Featherstone Creek. But what would I do if I found something shady about my own family? Would I bury the truth?

And as if on cue, I felt a little tickle in my nose.

Victoria.

I hadn't said a word, but she knew even when I was *thinking* about lying. I got her signal. Any attempts at burying the truth would be noted—and, most likely, punished.

I got home from school, tired from my research on the big secret. I had to dig into the local library's online archives and strained my eyes reading tiny digital versions of all those old documents. I didn't find any new information about the founding of the town—it was always the same story: Black-founded, Black-owned, and the same family names popped up over and over again. I had homework that would take at least an hour, and that was without snacks and dinner in between. Just as I took out my notes for math, Blake texted me:

BLAKE: How you feeling about the trip?

JUNE: A little 🫣, a little 😬. Do people still hate me or what? 😀

BLAKE: No one's talking about you that I know. People are over it. You do your math homework yet?

JUNE: Just started.

BLAKE: Concentrate on that and not the gossip. And pack when you're done.

I took her advice and turned back to my math textbook.

After finishing the math homework (and texting Blake to check my work), I closed my books and fell back on my bed. I looked up at the ceiling and pondered the rumors about Featherstone Creek. It had been a full day. Nia had started speaking to me again. The big scoop for the paper was becoming bigger and more challenging than I expected. And this camping trip was getting closer, about a week away. My mind started to race. So much was going on.

I grabbed my journal from under the mattress, hopped back over to my desk, and grabbed the key from behind the picture frame. I thought back to the beginning of the school year, when I felt so overwhelmed all the time about school, extracurriculars, and friend drama that I started having anxiety symptoms. I'd been getting better at managing it,  especially during the school musical—the singing really calmed me—but my fear about the camping trip was making my heart race again. I hopped onto my bed and began to write.

Dear Journal,

I just want to be liked again. By everyone. I want the camping trip to be drama-free. I want to crack this story about Featherstone Creek before Quincy and Tasha impress Ms. West and the entire school. Maybe then everyone would be so impressed by my work that they'd like me again! I want things to be back to normal. I want things to be normal with Nia and Lee and everyone. I want to . . . not have a headache! Breathe, June. Reeeeeelax. . . . Think about happy things. . . . Alvin . . . cupcakes . . . Okay, better . . .

Then the ceiling started to look weird, like a fog had rolled in from outside. The fog grew thicker. Maybe I was just tired from the day? The fog grew so thick that it came down on me like a blanket. I closed my eyes. Maybe they were playing tricks on me.

I opened my eyes again. The fog was gone. I sat up in bed, and I instantly knew where the fog had gone. It had transformed into Victoria, who was sitting at my desk.

"Busy day, June!" she said in a chipper tone. "We have to catch up after all that's happened."

I rolled my eyes. There's a big difference between best-friend-I-want-to-talk-to-every-day and fairy-godmother-I-never-asked-to-have. I didn't want to catch up with Victoria! She was like a parent. Usually she just came to scold me or to catch me in a lie or some other untruthful behavior. But I didn't think I'd done anything wrong today, or anything else to warrant her attention.

"I didn't even lie today!" I told her defensively.

"Nope, today you were pretty good," Victoria said. "But let's recap. You and Nia, speaking. That's huge!"

"Yeah," I said, scooting to the end of my bed and crossing my legs. "I was surprised. Do you think she's not mad at me anymore?"

"Hard to say," Victoria said. "Are you still mad at her?"

"Yeah," I said, nodding. Then I had another thought. "Maybe not *as* mad. But still mad."

Victoria nodded. "A good start. Now, don't forget, on the camping trip, it's your duty to apologize to as many people as possible. That's the only way I'll lift the spell.

Maybe other people are not as mad at you anymore, either. Maybe they'll be relieved to speak to you again."

I shrugged. I thought back to lunch today, how everyone was chatting like old times. It felt normal. It felt pre–blog leak.

Victoria gave me an encouraging pat on the knee. "And this story for the newspaper . . . are you really on the heels of something big?"

"I don't know," I said. "Depends on what I find out."

"Right," Victoria said. "Well, remember what Ms. West said. 'Be thorough. Be truthful.' "

I looked at her, surprised. "You were there for that meeting?"

"Of course," Victoria said. "I'm everywhere."

"Are you in all my classes every day?" I asked.

Victoria stood up. "Now, after all this time, you know I can't make myself known all the time. But I am always listening, and I pop up when you most need me."

It was that trait that frustrated me most.

"Now, my dear, you've had a big day. Get some rest."

And with that, Victoria stood in the middle of my room while the sparkly fog swirled around her, getting thicker and thicker until it eventually carried her away into thin air, leaving me alone in my room, ready to tuck into bed and finally call it a night.

CHAPTER SIX

✦✦
✦

On Friday, my mom decided we should go shopping for extra outdoor gear so I'd be as cozy and warm as possible. "Let's go downtown," Mom said. "There's an OUTPost there, and we can get you a fleece jacket. Maybe some other school things, if you're lucky."

"I'm down," I said. At least the camping trip was a good reason to go shopping.

Since Atlanta was about a forty-five-minute drive away, Mom decided to make a weekend of it. She booked us a hotel room downtown so we could shop and then have a nice dinner afterward without having to rush home through traffic. "Girls' trip!" I exclaimed when she told me.

Saturday was bright and sunny. We drove to the city in

the morning and listened to Mom's nineties hip-hop play-list on the way. (It was basically Jermaine Dupri's greatest hits, as every song on there was produced by him.)

Atlanta, to me, was where the action was. Big build-ings, wide streets, and busy people having meetings and closing deals and going out and doing important things. Businesses, government headquarters . . . movies were filmed here! This could be the first trip of many once I started acting. "You know, I'll have to start seeing agents here soon," I reminded Mom. "For my acting career."

"Riiiiight," my mom said slowly. "You sure you want to continue acting? Have you thought about doing anything behind the scenes? Since you like writing and you're on the school paper, you ever think about screenwriting? Maybe you can write a one-woman play," Mom said. "Playwriting is how Tyler Perry started."

"You think?" I said. I hadn't tried writing any works of my own yet. After my *Wiz* performance, I thought I was made for the stage. "I could write my own material for me to perform onstage. Maybe I should start auditioning for theaters in Atlanta."

Mom looked at me quickly. "But what about the paper and field hockey? You're pretty booked as it is."

"I'll manage," I said. At least, I believed I would manage. I was constantly trying to balance my schoolwork along-side my after-school activities. I liked being busy. I liked

other people, like my parents and my friends, to think of me as busy and able to do it all. But sometimes it was too much, and I got overwhelmed and panicked about how I could get everything done. That's probably what had led to me getting my first C plus ever in my math class this year—trying to do everything, not taking enough time to study or tell someone I needed help. Once I'd told Blake I was struggling, she helped me study and get my grade up. I knew I had to be better about managing my many responsibilities. And asking for help. Sigh. Everyone needed help sometimes. And it wasn't necessarily a bad thing. *Heck, even Beyoncé has assistants,* I thought. "Maybe I go for auditions in the summer, when school's out," I offered.

"Ah, right," my mom said, looking straight ahead. She turned up the dial on the car stereo and started singing along to some song where Diddy kept interrupting with "uh-huh, yeah" every two seconds. I looked out the window and watched cars switching lanes and speeding along as we approached downtown Atlanta. We turned off the highway and followed the directions on Google Maps toward the shopping district. I felt a flutter in my stomach, excited for the day ahead.

The OUTPost was a huge store for outdoor goods, located in the Plaza Mall in downtown Atlanta. Mom figured it would have the best selection of waterproof everything. I wasn't sure if I'd need my own tent for this trip. Or my own kayak. But if I did, this store sold both.

I meandered through the aisles, looking at the boots, fishing gear, tackle, camping tents, and sleeping bags. I picked up a thermos—the tag said it was "made of stainless steel and guaranteed to keep beverages and food warm in −30 degree weather." If it's that cold, should you even be sleeping outside? No thanks!

As I moved one of the sleeping bags out of the way to study another, I heard a female voice. "Can I help you with something?" said an older white saleswoman wearing a blue polo shirt and a nametag that read "Ginny."

"No, I'm just browsing," I replied. "I'm looking for camping clothes."

"Well, you're in the wrong section," the woman said. "Clothes are upstairs."

"Ah, okay," I said, and started to head for the stairs.

Just then my mom came toward me. "June, I've got to take this call outside. I'll be just a minute," she said.

As Mom turned away toward the door, I climbed the stairs alone. I noticed that the older store worker with the not-so-nice voice followed.

I spotted racks of coats and fleece pants on display in the middle of the second floor. Most of them were neutral, darker colors. A few pink-and-gray Patagonia fleece jackets caught my eye. I picked one up and tried it on, posing before a mirror to see the fit.

"Dear, that jacket costs one hundred dollars," the woman said from behind me.

I jerked my head around and met her eyes, which narrowed. I looked down at the tag on the sleeve. Indeed, the price was $99.99.

"Thanks," I said. "I can read the tag—I'm in the sixth grade!"

Ginny did not find the joke funny. "We don't tolerate stealing here," she continued.

My legs felt like concrete blocks in my shoes. My fists started to ball up involuntarily. I felt heat rise to my head. Was this happening? That thing I had heard about on television, watched in episodes of family TV shows, and read about on Instagram feeds—the thing that happens when Black girls go shopping? This was now happening to me, all alone, in Atlanta, at a camping goods shop, because apparently an eleven-year-old girl couldn't possibly need goods for a school camping trip, much less a 100 percent recycled polyester fleece jacket.

Because I was Black, because I knew I wasn't going to steal, because I knew this woman was out of line, and because I was under the truth-telling spell of Victoria, I blurted out the first thing that popped into my head.

"But apparently you tolerate racism!" I exclaimed.

Yup, I said it.

Ginny stood there, her mouth agape. I stood there, my eyes wide and fixed on her. I didn't move. She didn't move. I knew no matter what happened next, Ginny would be a part of my memory from this moment on.

Suddenly Mom appeared behind the woman, breaking my rage daze. "What's going on?" she asked.

I looked at the saleswoman. She looked at my mother.

"Nothing," Ginny said. "She was just trying on one of our jackets."

"Nothing?!" I yelled. I felt a vein popping in my forehead. "Nothing?! You just followed me around the store and then accused me of trying to steal!"

"Excuse me! I did not!" Ginny denied. "I just told you how much the jacket cost."

"But I didn't ask, because I could clearly see the price on the tag. You said you thought I was trying to steal it. Just admit it!"

My mother's eyes grew wide.

"Okay, hold on," the woman said, trying to smooth things over.

Mom looked at me, then at the saleswoman. My mom knew in an instant what had happened. She knew that in the two minutes she had left her daughter alone, she had exposed her to the malicious intentions of white people who get uncomfortable with Black people looking at expensive goods in stores. "June, take the jacket off."

I did what I was told. I was angry as I took it off. Did Mom not believe me? I was racially profiled in this stupid OUTPost store, and now my own mother wasn't going to believe me? I felt a burning sensation in my belly.

I handed my mother the fleece jacket. She folded it up and handed it to the woman.

"Listen, I'm sorry if she misunderstood—" the woman said.

"She didn't misunderstand a thing!" my mom said. "Come on, June."

We started walking toward the stairs as the woman beelined to a phone hanging behind a register. I turned around to watch her, but my mother grabbed my hand. "June, let's go." We walked quickly down the stairs.

We'd made it almost to the exit when another woman approached us. "Hi there. I'm Samantha. I manage the floor here," she said in this supercool, supersweet, and overly helpful tone, like she was about to escort me to the doctor's office for a checkup. "Can I do anything to help you?"

"Not a thing," my mom said quickly.

Samantha responded. "I understand my colleague Ginny upstairs may have made your daughter uncomfortable. I'm sorry about that."

My mother straightened up and looked Samantha in the eye. "What's sorry is how your sorry excuse for a co-worker treated my daughter. That's what's sorry."

"I, um, ma'am, I would be happy to get Ginny to come down here to apologize."

"The damage is already done," Mom said.

I noticed a few other shoppers looking in our direction, wondering what the commotion was about. Did they think I had stolen from the store? Were they as quick to judge me as racist Ginny was? What did they assume was going on with two Black women in this outdoor goods store having a testy conversation with manager Samantha? Were the cops going to come and make it all worse?

I pulled on my mother's hand. I wanted to leave—not out of shame but out of a need to put myself in a better place. I pulled her toward the exit, and Mom shifted her weight and followed me. "Let's go, Mom. There are better places to spend our money."

Mom opened the door for me, and I walked through. I didn't turn back once.

I didn't remember walking to the car. I didn't remember hearing anything. I didn't hear the chatter of other people on the sidewalk. Or my mother calling my name for the entire four-minute walk to the car. I heard a loud roar, like a train passing by, then chatter, but I couldn't make out any words. Once we got inside our car with the doors locked, the fury and anger that had grown in my belly spewed out of me in a primal sound that I imagined my mom only heard when her patients were in labor.

"June!" my mom finally called—or maybe had called earlier but I hadn't heard her. I grabbed my head, the freight train now screeching through my brain, giving me a headache. I felt the heat . . . the anger.

"Acccccccck!!!!" I screamed again.

"June!" Mom repeated. She looked panicked, as if she didn't recognize me or as if I had done something horrific. Her face was the first thing that had come into focus since we'd walked out of the store. Had I said something? Hurt anyone? And why was I breathing so hard? Had I been breathing like this for a while? Did I just run a race?

"June, honey, calm down," my mom kept repeating. "Just breathe! Breathe!"

"I'm breathing," I said, breathing quickly, like I couldn't gulp enough air.

"June, stay with me, breathe slower," she said, taking deep breaths with me. "Try to focus on something other than where we are. Let your mind go to a happy place, like on the stage at *The Wiz*."

I could feel my heartbeat through my hands. I tried to get my mind to focus, to stop thinking about the freight train and instead go somewhere more peaceful. "Breathe, June," my mom repeated. "One deep breath in"—I did as instructed—"and a deep breath out. Good."

I did this again and again until I could finally hear the traffic outside. My heartbeat started to slow down. My shirt was damp, sweaty. "What just happened?" I asked.

"I think you had a panic attack, honey," she said. "Probably triggered by what happened in the store."

"I've—I've never . . . ," I said.

"I know," Mom said. "But you breathed through it and you're fine now. You feel better?"

"Yeah," I said a bit breathlessly. "I just got so . . ."

"I know. Keep breathing. I'll get us out of here. Let's get some lunch and maybe you'll feel better."

We drove to a restaurant close by that looked like it had comfortable booths and dark lighting. I climbed slowly out of the car; my mom met me at the passenger's side before I could shut the door. She walked with her arm around my shoulders until we got seated inside at a table.

In Featherstone Creek, the Ginny thing would have never happened. Partly because 90 percent of the town was African American, partly because there weren't many white-owned businesses or white workers in Featherstone Creek, and partly because the white people who lived and worked there appreciated and respected Featherstone Creek's history and long-term residents. I'd been to very white towns before. We had to drive through some very white towns to get to Lake Lanier. I knew plenty of nice white people. I'd never experienced outright profiling like what had happened in the OUTPost store.

"June, darling, has this happened before?" Mom asked.

"What, the racism or the panic attack?" I asked.

"The, um . . . ," my mom said, speaking carefully. "What happened in the store. Let's start there."

"Yes, ma'am," I responded.

"To you?"

"Well, not really to me, but it does happen. I've heard of it happening."

"Where have you heard of it happening?"

"On the news, on TikTok. My friends have told me stories about when they've gone outside Featherstone Creek and they've been followed or someone's looked at them like they might steal something. It's, like, a feeling. A bad feeling."

"Yes, it's an awful feeling, one that I've tried to shield

you from for years. But it happens. And I hope it doesn't happen again, but something tells me it might."

"You're not going to tell Daddy, are you?" I said. I thought he'd be upset. "I just got on good terms with him again. I don't want to worry him with any of this."

"June, I hear you, but I have to tell your father. I don't keep secrets from him. And I want him to know this happened to you. What about if I ask him not to discuss it with you just yet? Would that work?"

"Fine," I said. Mom squeezed my hand.

We ate our food slowly, my mom giving my heart a chance to fully recover before we got moving again. By the end of lunch I felt more normal. The rage had mellowed, but I hadn't forgotten what happened. I couldn't forget that feeling of being suspected of stealing, suspected of doing something I couldn't even imagine doing. I tried to shake off Ginny's racist behavior, blaming her racism on her ignorance and not anything I did. But it didn't help—that burning sensation still irritated the inside of my stomach.

After lunch we pulled up to the front entrance of the hotel. My mom had a quick conversation with the valet, and then we walked inside to check in. After we unloaded our bags in the room and sat down for a few minutes, I pulled out my phone and started mindlessly looking up camping blogs on the internet. Perhaps I should have just shopped online for camping stuff. Then the whole Ginny disaster could have been avoided.

"So, feeling good about the trip?" Mom asked.

I gave an honest answer. "I'm a bit nervous, given everything happening with my friends. But I'll be all right. And thanks so much for taking me shopping, Mom." I gave her a hug and then went to the bathroom to get cleaned up.

I started to brush my teeth. I heard a simmering sound, like someone was shifting sand, and then I saw a foggy cloud rise up from the floor, though I hadn't yet showered. Suddenly a figure appeared in the mirror in front of me. Victoria.

"Hi, June," she said, stepping out of the mirror toward me, smoothing her dress and adjusting her tiara. "How are you doing?"

"I'm fine," I said. Actually, I was tired, too tired to deal with a Victoria lecture or her antics right now. But I knew she wasn't going to let me go. "What's up?"

"I'm checking on you. That was a pretty awful thing that happened to you today," she said. "Anyone else in your shoes probably would have reacted the same way."

"Well, I'm fine now," I said. I felt my lower lip quivering, but I refused to let racist Ginny make me cry. "But it's not fine what she did."

"I know. But I'm proud of you for standing up for yourself to that salesperson. She was completely out of line. And I'm proud of you for expressing yourself to your mom like you did."

"You're proud of me for having a panic attack?" I asked, confused.

"No, sweetie. I mean I'm proud of you for feeling your feelings but not letting your feelings consume you. That's what maturity is. That's what being a better person is. That's what I've been trying to teach you with the spell. If you want to cry, scream, or yell after what happened, you have every right to. It's okay to be mad when people treat you wrong. But, my dear, if that's the mental toughness you show in the face of the worst of humanity, I'm sure you can achieve anything."

Victoria cupped my chin in her hand. I looked up at her. She reminded me of my mother at times, soft and caring but encouraging. A smile grew across her face. "Remember, keep your head high, my dear, and don't let one shopkeeper's ignorance prevent you from entering another store. You belong wherever you are."

I nodded. I smiled back at her, relieved she wasn't going to punish me for anything I'd said today. If there

was a day of all days when I'd been truly honest about my feelings, it was today.

Victoria inched away from me toward the mirror, and suddenly she became transparent, like a ghost. Then a fog of fairy dust appeared across the mirror, and in an instant she was gone. I finished getting ready for bed, slathering on some body lotion, smiling at myself in the mirror. "Not today, Ginny, not today," I said to myself, and then left the bathroom to go to bed.

CHAPTER SEVEN

Though I had a decent night's sleep, I kept having mid-dream flashbacks to what had happened in the store. I shuddered at the thought of Ginny's voice. I didn't think I'd ever get that shrill sound out of my head. What if I got nervous about running into someone like Ginny at every store I went into?

"What if I'm too scared to go shopping for the rest of my life?" I asked my mom over breakfast at the hotel the next morning.

"I completely understand why you might feel that way," she said. "And it might take some time for that feeling to go away. But I was thinking of going to a different mall today. And no matter what happens, I will be right next to you, right there, to make sure my baby can exercise her right to shop just like anyone else."

I looked at my mom, with her broad smile and wide eyes. She wrapped her arms around me, and I instantly felt my shoulders relax. I thought back to what Victoria had said: *"You belong wherever you are."* I thought about Mom and driving to Atlanta yesterday, us laughing and talking while we listened to music. At least I knew the car ride to another mall would be a good time. "Okay," I said. "But, yeah, don't leave me this time."

She drove us to another mall, the Woods, that had an REI and some other shops. I braced myself as I walked in the door. Surprisingly, two spiky-haired boys named Jake and Tom came to help my mom and me. They spent a long time explaining something called Gore-Tex to the two of us and ran back and forth from the dressing room to the floor to fetch items for us to try on. They were nice, so nice that we walked out of there with three shopping bags' worth of stuff.

I came home with an amazing blue sleeping bag that promised to keep me warm in −50 degree weather. (I'm not hiking Mount Everest, but if I ever wanted to, I'd have a cozy place to sleep.) I also snagged a stainless-steel water bottle that Jake said would keep my drinks cold or soup hot for eight hours. Mom got me a new light-beige Fjällräven backpack and a pair of white Birkenstocks.

"Mom, these are on trend!" I told her.

"Well, I know what's cool," she said.

"You do?" I raised an eyebrow.

"Well, at least I know enough to look it up online."

Just a few months ago I'd cringed while she picked out outfits for me that belonged on school picture day for kindergarten. Now she was buying trendy stuff for me based on what she'd seen on the internet. I felt like we'd made progress. "Mom, we've come so far."

"Indeed," she said as we walked into the house. "I'll

be downstairs working on dinner. Don't forget to pack underwear," she said.

I went upstairs to my room and started folding clothes into small piles to tuck into my new backpack.

Monday afternoon, after I'd come home from school and gotten settled into my room to study, my phone vibrated.

CHLOE: U around?

I called her immediately. "Um, did I tell you what happened this weekend? We went shopping for this dang camping trip. And guess what? Some racist white lady accused me of stealing in the camping goods store."

"Wooowwwww, you serious?" Chloe responded.

I told Chloe the whole story. The anger in my voice bubbled up once again just retelling the story. It was like Ginny was in my bedroom, looking at me through the mirror.

"So typical, June! So typical! And so rude!" Chloe said. "But also, who still does that? Like, with everyone having cell phones and everyone so quick to record when Karens are being racist, like, why would she even try you?" Chloe said with a laugh.

"I don't think it's funny."

"What she did wasn't funny, but the fact that she did it and thought she wasn't going to get caught is just dumb," Chloe said. "Why didn't you record it?"

"I didn't think about it in the moment," I said. "I was too angry."

"Well, if it ever happens again, get it on video and up-load immediately," Chloe declared. "It'll go viral, and Karen or Ginny or whoever will get fired and *boom*. Justice served."

"I don't want to think about it anymore," I said, my temples starting to throb. "I gotta prepare for my apology tour in the woods."

"You think people are still worried about that blog?" Chloe said.

"Probably!"

"It's been, like, three weeks, and you wrote an apology in the paper!" Chloe said. "Keep it moving. It's over. I gotta jump. Text me later."

I hung up with Chloe, my head hurting from thinking about that run-in again. I hated that Ginny kept popping into my mind. It was like living the incident over again each time, even though I'd had a fine time at the REI store today. I hoped my mom wouldn't bring up the incident at dinner. I had to get downstairs before my dad got home, so I could stop my mom from telling him anything.

From the stairs I could smell butter and garlic, and I started to salivate. I heard my dad's voice as he talked with my mother about his day.

"Hey, Junebug, how's my baby girl?" he said to me as I entered the kitchen.

"All good." I felt an itch in my nose. Ugh, that darn Victoria. *Can't we sit down for dinner first before I tell my dad what happened?* I thought quickly before Victoria gave me an allergy attack. I had to say something truthful. Maybe I could quote a song lyric? Or make one up? "You know, sidestepping haters to get to something greater?" I rapped. Corny, I knew it.

"Is that a song?"

"It is now," I said. I backed away from him to set the table.

Mom and Dad and I dug into Mom's pasta with homemade tomato sauce and garlic bread. I ate quickly, still feeling a turning in my stomach over the shopping incident, then excused myself to go back to my room.

Over the next few days, I tried to throw myself into research and forget about the horrible shopping incident. I wanted to relax, but my mind kept going back to what had happened. I looked over at my shopping bags and gritted my teeth. I needed to let it go. I needed to distract myself by focusing on something else. I went to my computer and looked up the notes I had written for that newspaper article. The secret of Featherstone Creek.

I started googling Featherstone Creek's history again, looking up early settlers and businesses that were founded here. I skimmed through newspaper articles from our local paper and the *Atlanta Journal-Constitution*, and I even found my mom's family mentioned in a few of them. One article gave a brief history of the town's founding families. A lot of those families still lived nearby, and I figured I could interview them for my story when I was ready.

Then I found an article from 1926 about the first hospital founded in town:

The Featherstone Star

FEATHERSTONE CREEK MEDICAL INSTITUTE FOUNDED BY FOUR LOCAL DOCTORS

A new hospital in downtown Featherstone Creek founded by four residents opened yesterday on Main Street, bringing medical care to the growing population of the region. The medical facility will offer birthing, pediatric, and emergency-care services to residents of Featherstone and the surrounding towns. The doctors and nurses at the hospital have experience working throughout the South and graduated from the Glick School of Medicine in London.

I looked at the picture of the founders of the hospital that accompanied the article. The two male doctors in white lab coats were surrounded by three female nurses, and in the background was another man on horseback. I wondered if he was one of the women's husbands. He

didn't look familiar. I gave a shrug and saved the links for my notes.

I found some other notable news reports. The first general store here had been founded by a woman married to a general in the navy. A famous cabaret performer from the 1920s settled here after touring Europe and started Featherstone Creek's first dance school. Maybe she had some secrets! Who would settle in quiet Featherstone Creek after an exciting career in Europe? Maybe she was a spy? Recruited by some European spy organization to get intel on the United States? Maybe she wasn't American at all? I had to do more digging on her.

My vision had started to blur from tiredness, and my hand could barely move the cursor up to the text bar. I slapped my laptop lid closed and put to rest for the evening my search into the great mystery of Featherstone Creek. Maybe my truth-telling superpowers would finally do me some good and lead me to the biggest scoop of the year for the school newspaper. For now, I followed my true calling: my bed. I called it a night and fell fast asleep.

CHAPTER EIGHT

✦✦
✦

The time—Friday—had come to head to
the woods. I was prepared for anything nature could
throw at me. I had bug spray, a thermos, waterproof socks,
boots, and a hat. The only thing I didn't have was Hate-
Away, a spray that could prevent the entire Featherstone
Creek sixth grade from doing anything to hurt me.

My mom drove me to school with my gear in the car,
and helped me roll my oversized bag into the school auditorium. The class was supposed to check in there before
we loaded onto three coach buses to head to the camp.

I felt sweat bead on my upper lip as I saw other students gathering in the auditorium. No one looked my
way; all of them were lost in their own conversations.

"You have everything you need?" Mom asked.

"I think I'm good," I said. "Here's my phone, since I won't need it in the woods."

"I'll keep it safe. Love you, honey. Be good."

I heaved my bag up a few rows of the seats and sat down. I didn't have the energy to drag it any farther. I looked around and hoped to see Nia or Olive or someone who might want to hang out with me. Suddenly I heard a voice over my shoulder.

"You bring the s'mores?" Alvin asked.

My face instantly relaxed. Alvin had his backpack slung over one shoulder and a fishing pole in hand. I smirked and pointed at the pole. "I don't know if I'll need it, but we will be by a lake. I know Lee brought his," he said with a shrug.

I nodded. "I'm sure it will come in handy. You can catch us our dinner!" Corny jokes. Total signs of a crush. *Ugh, June, be chillll!*

He sat next to me and we pulled out our papers with details of the trip. The school had given us a map of the grounds, a schedule of our daily events, and a guide to our trip chaperones and advisors. I perked up when I saw that Ms. West had been assigned as our group's chaperone. At least someone I trusted would be watching over us in the woods.

I scanned the auditorium. Most of the kids had already arrived. I spotted Nia and Olive sitting together near the front row. My stomach dropped to my knees, and I wished I were there with them, but I was still keeping a safe distance from Nia. I didn't need the drama to start before the trip even began. I saw Lee walking across the auditorium toward Alvin and me. As Alvin had predicted, Lee held a fishing pole in his hand. He wore a flannel shirt over his baggy LeBron James T-shirt.

"What's good?" he said as he sat down next to Alvin. Lee gave me a cursory nod to be polite, but I could tell he really wanted to chat with his friend.

"Ready to hit these woods," Alvin said brightly.

Lee and Alvin continued chatting without including me in the conversation. But I was grateful for the nod—it was better than nothing. Through the crowd, smiles and laughter were all I saw.

A simmer of excitement filled the auditorium as Ms. West walked onstage. "All right, kids, who's ready to go camping?" she yelled. Everyone cheered. "Okay, let's make sure that we have all of our belongings. As you see from our schedule, we have a full itinerary of fun things for you over the weekend, so gather your things and let's start heading to the buses."

I loaded onto the second bus, with most kids filing in toward the back while parent and teacher chaperones stayed up front. I slid into an empty window seat. I wasn't intentionally trying to hide from anyone, but I thought my trip to the woods might go more smoothly if I kept a low profile until I got the courage to start my apology tour. I hoped no one would sit next to me, unless it was Alvin or Blake, so I could go unnoticed during the ride to the campground.

I stashed my backpack under the seat and watched as other kids excitedly loaded onto the bus. Nia boarded and gave a wave to a few well-dressed girls in the front of the bus. Of course Nia knew them—she somehow had always made friends with girls who looked like they were posing for Instagram at all times. A few other kids squeezed by her on the way to their seats. Then she sat down next to Olive—I could see Olive's hair above the seat two rows ahead of me.

Just then, Alvin reappeared in the aisle beside me. I gasped as he sat down in the seat next to me. "Is this seat taken?" he asked.

I stammered, "N-n-n-no! No! Of course not!" I said way too excitedly. I looked around and noticed that most

of the seats were full and the last of the parent chaperones were coming on board.

Ms. West stood in front of the aisle and addressed the entire bus. "All right, here we go. As a reminder, Lake Lanier is
a tech-free zone," she announced, "meaning you should not
have any cell phones or tablets or laptops with you. There's
very little Wi-Fi out in the woods, anyway. You have a journal assignment for your first day, to write down any fears
you might have of the woods and how you think you can
work through them. We'll be there in about an hour."

We started moving, and I held on tight to my notebook, careful not to lose it on the bus. Now that I was
keeping all my secrets in my journal, I needed to keep it
as close and as secret as possible. I couldn't have someone
find it—I'd have Leak 2.0 to deal with. I turned to a fresh,
clean page. I wrote:

My Biggest Fears of the Woods

- Being kidnapped by an angry sixth grader
- Being left in the woods naked and afraid
- Having someone find this diary
- Being alone in the dark
- Having to use the restroom (are there outhouses
  out there?!)

Just then Alvin looked over. "You scared of the dark?" he said.

"No!" I spat out. Was that true? I was scared of being in the dark with this crowd since the blog disaster, that was for sure. I felt a tingle in my nose. "Um, well, I dunno," I responded. "Not usually."

"You're scared," Alvin said.

"No!" I said again. My nose got itchier. "I'm just not really a sleep-outside-with-the-bugs person."

Alvin looked at me. He saw the journal in my lap, then looked up at my eyes. *Oh, please don't say anything about the blog. Please don't ask. Pleeeeeaasssee . . .*

"It's all right," Alvin said. "Your secret's safe with me."

OMG.

What does that mean? Which secret? The one about being scared of the dark? Did he see what I wrote in my journal? Or did he know I got all weird and blushy every time he was around me? Did he think I liked him? Did he know he might be right?

I couldn't concentrate on the journal assignment after that; I slapped the book shut and put it away. Alvin yammered on with Lee, who sat across the aisle from us, about fish and dirt and creek stuff. I dissected Alvin's words in my head for the entire hour-long ride while the rest of the sixth grade cackled and sang their way to the campsite. I still had little faith that this camping trip was a good idea, spell or no spell.

✦

We arrived at the campsite and spilled out of the buses onto the grounds. Students filtered into their assigned cabins and looked for their cabinmates. I was in cabin 1, located in the middle of the campground in sight of the main entrance. Olive followed behind me, and I was relieved to share a cabin with someone who had my back. At least a little of my back. As opposed to someone who didn't care whether I was abducted by bears.

Blake walked up behind us a few minutes later. "Is this one?" she asked.

Okay, this trip was not going to completely stink. "Yes! Let's go pick our beds."

We placed our backpacks down on two sets of bunk beds. There was room for another girl, and I felt a nervous tingle in my chest. "Is Nia in this cabin?" I asked.

"I don't think so," Olive said. "She said she was in two. Think that's across from us. She walked ahead of me when we got off the bus."

I looked at the empty bed and was surprised to feel a small pang of disappointment. At least I wouldn't be sleeping next to an enemy.

Just then our parent chaperone, Ms. Johnston, popped her head into our room. "Girls, we need to head to the main lodge for the all-camp assembly and lunch."

A face peeked in behind her—Rachelle, who announced, "Guys, I'm in this cabin, too!"

"That means you round out the group of four," Ms. Johnston said. "Put your stuff down, honey, and then we can head out."

"I'm starving," Blake said. "Let's go."

We quickly followed our chaperone up the hill to the main lodge, which was already buzzing with kids squealing and laughing. We filed inside to line up for lunch. I grabbed a lunch tray and trailed behind Olive, picking up a turkey sandwich, a bag of baked chips, and a fruit cup. We took a table nearby and sat down.

Ms. West blew a whistle, and the room fell quiet. "All right, campers, let's go over a few things. Remember, stay with your group. You're only allowed inside your own cabin—no visiting anybody else's—and you must be inside for roll call after dinner, at eight p.m."

I looked around the cafeteria as kids ate and took in their new surroundings. Students chattered excitedly, thrilled to be away from school and parents. I was thinking about how and when I was going to apologize to all these distracted sixth graders, who wanted nothing more than to run free in the woods and get away from me.

After lunch we broke into our separate groups, and I joined the other people in the K group, including Alvin. Ms. West reviewed some of the activities for the next few days. Alvin shot me a look as she described the games, and Rachelle took copious notes. I nodded slowly and looked on, but I didn't take out my journal until we headed back to the bunk to unpack and settle in.

Once there, I waited until Olive, Blake, and Rachelle were busy either changing clothes or gossiping to get my journal out of my bag and start writing:

Dear Journal,

My apology tour needs to start now. What's the best way to begin? Grab a megaphone and scream "I'M SORRY!!!" over the campground? That would be the easiest way to do it. But I know Victoria would want something more . . . personal. Sigh. . . . it's going to be hard. The entire class treats me like I'm invisible. It's like they all forgot I was the lead in the school play. I know—I'll start at breakfast tomorrow. Wonder what's on the menu? Will we have to cook the food ourselves? Can we have pancakes like at any normal sleepover???

CHAPTER NINE

✦✦
✦

Saturday morning, I left my cabin early so I could find my water bottle, which I needed for our morning hike. Everyone was due to meet at the main lodge for a long trek around the lake. We'd take notes on the various bugs and plants we found.

Dressed in sweatpants, I quickly looked around the grounds and spotted the water bottle by the entrance to the main lodge. I double-timed it back to my cabin to finish getting ready. When I was almost at the entrance, I saw Nia out of the corner of my eye. She was standing at the door of the cabin opposite mine. I held my breath. She looked up just as I looked up. We had nowhere to hide.

"Hi," she said.

"Hi," I said.

The pause between us seemed to go on forever. I felt like I could hear every animal in the woods calling to me in the time it took for Nia to find her next words. "You sleeping in one?"

"Yeah," I said. "You in two?"

"Yeah," she said. "There's no hot water. No idea how I'm going to shower in there."

"There's always the creek," I said. That sounded . . . weird. But after what she'd done to me, I felt like she should bathe in the creek with the reptiles and other critters. Still, I felt horrible the second the words came out of my mouth. Was I really telling my one-time best friend to jump in a creek? I knew Victoria wasn't going to like that.

"Anyway, how's, like, stuff?" I asked in a weak attempt to change the subject and make small talk.

"It's fine," Nia said coolly. "You?"

"Good," I said. That wasn't a lie. "Great!" I said even more enthusiastically. Maybe that was a stretch. I felt a tickle in my nose.

I didn't want to have a long conversation with Nia, with the potential for more lies to spew out. I also didn't know if I could handle her going off on me right now, alone, about the blog, about Lee, about everything. Was this where we were going to have our knock-down, drag-out fight? Right here alone in the woods, where no one could see us or save us or pull us apart? I wasn't ready.

But I had to apologize. To everyone. EVERYONE, according to Victoria, or else I wouldn't get the spell lifted. I had to say something.

"I'm . . . um . . . ," I started.

"I gotta change shoes for this hike," Nia said. "See you." She turned on her heel and went inside her cabin. I didn't even have a chance to apologize. I watched her walk away, my mouth still open, trying to form words, even though no one was around to hear them. I couldn't get out "I'm sorry" in time, but at least I'd tried. I was ready to offer an apology. But was Nia ready to hear it?

◆

My legs were shaky at the beginning of our hike around Lake Lanier. We would head even deeper into the woods, away from the campsite, and I worried about what might happen to me out there. Like, who would trip me and cause me to fall over the safety railing and down an embankment? (Knew I should have packed safety rope in my backpack!) But once we got moving, I started to relax. I fell in step with the rest of the sixth-grade class as we marched along the trail that wound around the creek and deeper into the forest. It was quiet—only birds chirping and wind breezing through the leaves. Someone started a sing-along to "A-marching We Will Go." I studied the trees as I walked. I wondered how tall they were, how long they must have been growing alongside this lake, how many more acres of woods there might still be if people hadn't come in and built lodges and cleared space for camper vans and RVs.

The air smelled damp but clean. Lee and Alvin were walking ahead of me, and I kept my eyes on them when I wasn't looking at the flora and fauna or taking notes for

our school project. Twenty minutes in, I was more concerned with the number of shades of green I saw than who was thinking about me. Maybe I should do this hiking thing more often.

At one point, we had to cross a bridge over the creek, which required a few people to hold the bridge steady and give a hand so that others could pass. That's where that spark of fear re-entered my soul. I was scared that nobody would help me over and the sixth grade would walk ahead and head back to camp and leave me out by the river alone, wet, damp, and cold. But I saw Rachelle give a wave to Lee, Alvin, and Marcus Jones, who was tall and stocky and played on the football team, to make sure that I made it over safely. Marcus and Lee, along with two chaperones, held the bridge steady as I walked across it, and Alvin reached out his hand to help me take that last step to the other side. "Thank you," I said politely to all of them, looking directly into their eyes. All three guys gave me a nod.

After the hike, we headed back to our cabins and got cleaned up for dinner. I picked small balls of pollen off my jacket and unpacked my things. There were two showers and four of us in the cabin, so I waited my turn, taking out my journal and writing down some thoughts before I hopped in.

Dear Journal,

Okay, that wasn't too bad. Made it through a trek in the woods and survived. No one booby-trapped me. Alvin, Marcus, and Lee helped me over the bridge, and dare I say I caught a nice word from Rachelle? Maybe I will make it out of here without injury. Anyway, so far, so good. But time is ticking, and I need to start my apology tour soon. Who should I start with? Rachelle? Would that be weird? I tried to apologize to Nia, but she cut me off. Maybe I should start with Olive, even though she's already speaking to me. Practice run?

When Olive got out of the shower, I was sitting on my bed. I looked at her and said awkwardly, "I'm . . . I'm sorry again about the blog."

"Girl, you've said that a million times," she responded, rolling her eyes. "You're forgiven—it's done."

I glanced at her again, then sheepishly turned away. I looked down at my lap. "I'm just . . . it's hard. I'm just trying to make it right with people, and I want to make it right with everyone."

"Wasn't writing that column enough?" Olive said.

"Not if people are still mad at me."

Olive looked at me. "Who's still mad? Nia? So far it seems people are more concerned about the mosquitoes than about you and your blog. What's up with that blog, anyway? Did you delete it?"

"Yeah, I had to!" I said. "I couldn't have anyone, including me, see it anymore."

"Well, that's one way to get people to forgive you," Olive said, smiling. "Why don't you start apologizing at dinner? I'll be there to back you up."

"For real?"

"Yeah," Olive said. "I'll be your apology hype girl."

Dinner was served in the main lodge. Olive, Blake, Rachelle, and I walked over together from the cabin with Ms. Johnston. I put on the fleece jacket I had bought at REI, Blake had on an oversized Adidas sweatshirt, and Olive and Rachelle were wearing large flannel shirt jackets. ("Shackets," Rachelle informed us. "Kind of a shirt, kind of a jacket.") We walked close together to stay warm; the breeze felt a bit colder and damper without the sun to warm the air. The stars and the lights of the lodge began to peep through the dark haze of the night.

Inside the lodge, the clinking of silverware against plates and bowls echoed throughout the large room. The entire class gathered at the picnic tables and enjoyed a yummy pot of chili with a side of cornbread. Blake and

Rachelle found seats for the four of us at the end of a long table. I saw Nia sitting with Erica and Keisha at a table in the corner, nodding and chatting away.

I thought about going up to people to start apologizing. I looked for kids who weren't deep in conversation or with large groups. But everyone was either eating or talking, and after they finished, they bolted from the dining room to gather around a large campfire and make s'mores. Dang, I'd blown my chance. I silently begged Victoria not to give me a sneezing fit around the fire. I might put the flames out!

Outside, we huddled under blankets laid out on logs and inflatable cushions. Olive and Blake and I sat together, Alvin sat near Rachelle, and Ms. West sat opposite us. When everyone had sticky fingers from roasting their marshmallows, Quincy got our attention. "Does anyone know the tale of Left-Eye Louie?" he started. I wondered if he was part of the Featherstone Creek founder mystery.

"Left-Eye Louie was one of the first residents around the creek. That is, until one Friday the thirteenth, when he had the accident," Quincy continued. "Lost an eye, and his life shortly after, but many say his spirit still lives on around these woods."

I stopped chewing my s'more. Olive and I looked at each other, eyes wide. "His spirit lives on?" I asked. "What, meaning his ghost is around here somewhere?"

"Some have said," Quincy replied. "I've never seen him, but maybe . . . he could be around."

Great, so now we've got the ghost of some one-eyed farmer to worry about? How am I supposed to sleep tonight?

In all my years of going to Lake Lanier, I'd never heard this rumor. Why hadn't my parents told me to watch out for this old man whenever Lee and I went to the creek? I looked around the fire for Lee to see if I could ask him, or at least see his reaction to the story. His eyes were wide, and he smacked on his dessert with interest.

"So is he dead, or sort of dead?" someone asked.

"He was," Quincy said. "But he's been seen around."

"Is he mean?" someone else asked.

"Well, he's not too happy about missing an eye, that's for sure."

We all sat silent for a few moments. Olive pulled her knees in tight to her chest and wrapped her arms around her legs. Nia gave Ms. West a side-eye. Alvin scratched his face. The rest of the class looked at Quincy with wide eyes, skeptical but still nervous about Left-Eye Louie being real.

Ms. West broke the silence. "I've never seen Left-Eye Louie, and I've been coming to this lake longer than most of you have been alive. I have heard he only goes after people who litter in the park or leave it worse than they found it. So if we're respectful of our natural surroundings and pick up our trash, we should be fine."

Wow, only Ms. West could turn a horror story into a PSA on littering. We all looked at each other and laughed nervously. Then we tossed the chocolate bar wrappers into the trash bins and the graham cracker boxes into recycling. We folded up our blankets in neat piles and made sure we didn't leave any signs that we'd gathered there, both to save the planet and to (potentially) save ourselves from Left-Eye Louie. (If he existed. But he didn't. But just in case.)

"Nice work, guys. Left-Eye Louie won't be anywhere near these parts," Ms. West said. I hoped she was right.

After we'd finished cleaning up the s'mores party, we had to report to our cabins for bedtime. I nervously looked around as I gathered my things at the campfire site.

"Want me to walk you back?" Alvin suggested. "Protect you from Left-Eye Louie?"

"Oh-em-gee, yes, please," I said. I didn't care if he knew I was shaking in my Timberlands after that story. My pulse was twenty beats faster than normal, and I absolutely wanted someone to watch my back until I got to my bunk.

We started walking together in the dim light. It seemed like we were the last ones around. Either people were in the main lodge grabbing some of the few leftover chocolate chip cookies or they were already back in their cabins. "You're not still nervous about him, are you? He doesn't exist," Alvin said, interrupting my thoughts.

"No!" I said quickly. My nose started to itch, and I suddenly had a strong urge to sneeze. Okay, that was a lie. I was kinda scared. "Well, um, maybe . . . how do you know he doesn't exist?" I said.

"Wouldn't you have heard about him before now?" Alvin said. "How long have you and your family been coming to this lake? Lee, too? All this time and not one of you has heard about the dude? Something ain't right."

Maybe he was right. I mean, Lee of all people would have known if there was a ghost walking around Lake Lanier. "You've never heard anything about this before?"

"Nope, and you know I would have found him if he was here."

My pulse started to slow. Alvin's theory made sense. It was just a fireside tale to entertain us. "You're probably right," I said, and laughed nervously.

When we got to the door of my cabin, I looked at Alvin. He was smiling but seemed to be searching for the words to tell me something.

"Thanks for walking me home," I said. "I needed a zombie guard."

"Anytime," Alvin said. He paused.

I pivoted toward my door, and he called, "June!"

I turned back and looked directly into his eyes. He looked shy, like he knew something and was scared to tell me. "What's up?"

He took a breath. "I really like hanging with you, June."

"I—um, I—" My heart jumped again. I had to say something, anything. I should've told him I had feelings, that I'd liked him, too, ever since the musical. Words came up through my throat. My body was willing me to tell the truth. I hoped Victoria was watching!

Without hesitating, I told him how I felt.

"Right back atcha!" I said, and instantly cringed.

Um, that did not come out how I thought it would. It sounded unromantic. Dorky.

Alvin started to back away, a bit confused. Oh man, had I just hurt his feelings? Did he think I just friend-zoned him? Argh!

"I, um . . . ," I said. *I . . . um . . . really made a mess of that!* is what I thought.

"A'ight, I'll . . . um . . . I should go," Alvin said, quickly backing away from my door. I was tongue-tied. I wanted to call out to him, explain myself, say that "right back atcha" was my way of saying "Yes, I like you, too, a lot!"—and not in the I-like-guacamole-on-my-tacos way but in the serious, I-like-you-as-a-human-being-I-want-to-spend-more-time-with way. But I couldn't get all of that out of my mouth in time. And now Alvin was already halfway to his cabin, all before I could explain myself.

How in the world had I bungled that so badly? All I'd had to do was . . . *tell the truth.*

I walked into the cabin and plopped down on my bed. Maybe the other girls were still at the lodge, or at least my mind was so preoccupied that I didn't notice if anyone else was around. I didn't know what to make of the Alvin comment. *Right back atcha?* What did that even mean? Had I really said that? Why was I stumbling over myself?

Just then I heard a knock on the door, and Ms. Johnston popped her head in. "Hi, June, just checking in."

"All good," I said. But then she came in and took a seat on the end of my bed. I recognized the glimmer in her eyes, and then I saw it—the flutter of fairy dust falling off her shoulders. She began to transform into someone else before my eyes, swapping out a flannel jacket and chinos for the ball gown and tiara of a fairy godmother. Victoria! Always popping up when I least expected it.

"Oh, dear June!" she said brightly. "So that exchange with Alvin was quite interesting. He confessed his true feelings for you, and you, um, sort of did the same?"

"I goofed, I know," I said. "But I didn't lie."

"No, you most certainly didn't," Victoria joked. "I'm proud of you for that! So what happens now? Are you going to tell him how you really feel?"

"I have no idea," I said, slinking deeper under my sheets. "I'll probably avoid him until we go home."

"Ah, don't fret, my pet. Just be honest with him. Honesty is your strong suit."

It certainly didn't feel that way right then.

"And what's going on with Nia?" Victoria said.

"Nothing. It's whatever." *It's actually confusing, that's what it is.*

"Well, it needs to be more than whatever. As you mentioned to your friend Olive, you're supposed to be apologizing to your classmates one by one while you're here. Don't forget!"

"It's impossible to forget you and your spell, Victoria."

"Good! That's my girl!" She stood and started to turn around quickly. She kicked up quite a mess—first dirt, then thick matter, then a tornado, until she wafted into thin air and disappeared. At that moment, Blake and Olive stepped out from the bathroom, their toothbrushes in hand. They looked at me, confused expressions on their faces.

"What just happened?" Olive asked.

CHAPTER TEN

✦ ✦
✦

"I'll tell you what just happened," I said to Olive as she stood there holding a tube of toothpaste. "I basically guaranteed I will never, ever have another guy friend so long as I live."

"All this while we were in the bathroom?" Olive asked.

Rachelle heard us chatting and came in from the bathroom to see what the fuss was about. I told them what had gone down with the Alvin situation, including my ridiculous catchphrase. Rachelle tried, unsuccessfully, to hold in laughter. Olive blinked as she listened to my response. "'Right back atcha?' That's the worst thing you could have said to him!"

"Well, I didn't know what to say!" I said, pulling the blanket from my bed over my head for dramatic effect. "I

was still scared thinking about stupid Left-Eye Louie, and then Alvin drops that news. I wasn't ready!"

The girls were cracking up over my brutal honesty. This was why I'd usually been too afraid to share my feelings about deep things before. Ridicule, mockery. But as they laughed, I began to laugh, too. I mean, it was so corny that it was funny. And it wasn't like I'd been mean to him or cruel or anything. I'd just put my foot in my mouth!

Olive and Blake sat next to me on the bed and looked at me like I was an adorable puppy that had just accidentally chewed on their favorite shoes.

"I get you," Olive said. "I probably would have done the same thing. You're looking around to make sure someone-eyed ghost isn't trying to get you, and he's trying to confess his feelings. I'd have been shook, too."

"What do I do now?" I asked.

"Next time you see him, tell him how you feel," Blake said. "Do you know how you feel?"

"Um, maybe, kinda, sorta?"

"Then that's what you say," Blake said. "I maybe, kinda, sorta like you."

"That sounds worse than 'right back atcha,'" I replied.

We stayed up figuring out how best to explain to Alvin what I was feeling ("Rap it! 'I have feelings of feelings, but I don't know how to reveal what I'm feeling!'" Olive joked while Rachelle beatboxed to the words.) Laughs were had until the real Ms. Johnston—I didn't see any fairy dust, so I knew it was her—came around and told us it was lights-out. I went to sleep feeling reconnected with friends just like old times, pre–blog leak. My truth-telling fail was exactly what I'd needed.

◆

Dear Journal,

No one's coming for my head quite yet. Ms. West did try to freak everybody out with that story about Left-Eye Louie, but Alvin calmed me down and had a good reason for why Left-Eye Louie doesn't exist. I believe him over Ms. West. Alvin also told me he liked me on the way back to the cabin, and I, like a fool, told him "right back atcha." Might as well have complimented him on his ankles. He probably won't speak to me for the rest of this trip. I mean, I wouldn't speak to me, either.

Speaking of speaking, I have to start apologizing to people. No chickening out—just do it. Be brave, be sorry, and move on! #endthespell #thetruthwillsetyoufree

Sunday morning, everyone woke up in one piece. We all said silent prayers of gratitude that no one had been visited in the middle of the night by Left-Eye Louie. We had a full day's schedule of games and activities, like learning to compost trash. After breakfast, there was a fishing outing. (Alvin had been right to bring his fishing pole, but the camp also provided poles for us.) I had fished before, a bunch of times up here with Lee.

I missed those days. He'd put the worm on my hook for me because I was too grossed out and felt too guilty hurting the worm. I looked around for him as we got separated into groups to take various positions on the docks overlooking the lake. Lee was in a different group, on a dock farthest to the left. Sigh.

I stood with Olive and Blake on our dock with my fishing pole, bopping my hook into the water as I hoped for the big catch. The lake was quite soothing, even with a few dozen students standing on the dock. The water rippled as our hooks broke the surface. The lush sounds of birds singing and leaves blowing in the breeze calmed my nerves. I looked around at the other kids and saw a collective sense of both concentration and curiosity. School—its existence, its homework, and its drama, including my disastrous blog scandal—was a zillion miles away.

I made it through the morning activities without a panic attack, without someone throwing me into the water, and without falling off the dock into the lake. I even caught a fish. (Okay, it was a guppy. It was basically someone else's minnow. But it nibbled on my hook, and I pulled it out of the water. I threw it back immediately, since Ms. West said we shouldn't harm the delicate lake ecosystem by taking the fish.)

It really seemed like people had forgotten about that horrible blog. Or at least they were focused on more peaceful things in our rural surroundings. I figured lunchtime would be a great time to start my apology tour—it was when people would probably be most calm. I started with Marcus. Since he had helped me cross the bridge yesterday, I thought he might be the least mad at me still. I spotted him in the line for soup. "Hey," I said, getting his attention. "So I, um, just wanted to say, uh . . . that I was sorry, you know . . . about that blog thing." I clenched my teeth. The moment of truth. Would my apology work?

He looked at me, confused. "Okay," he said. And nothing more.

I said more. "Really. I am. Truly. Sorry."

"Okay," he said, unbothered. "You getting soup?"

It was a non-reaction to my apology. That was good. Right? "Um, yeah yeah yeah . . ." He scooted over so I could reach for a small cup of soup, then slid down the line to grab crackers. Nothing more was said.

Not so bad, I thought. *Who's next?*

As I walked up to the beverage station, I saw Carmen Evans. I had said some petty things about her messing up the dance steps in rehearsals for *The Wiz*, even though she still did a great job in the actual show. I noticed the plaid hiking boots she had on. Those could help me break the ice. "I like your boots," I told her.

"Thanks," she said. "Love that jacket."

"Yeah, thank you!"

Ice broken. Here goes.

"Carmen, I'm sorry for what I said about you in my blog. It was harsh, and you did an amazing job in *The Wiz*. I just wanted you to know that. From me personally."

She looked at me and pursed her lips. "Okay, June. Apology accepted."

I exhaled. "I'm really sorry."

"It's okay," she said, crossing her arms. "I said some bad stuff about you when I read that blog. So let's just call it even."

I'd take that. "Even."

"And tell me where you got that jacket, 'cause I might wanna buy one."

I laughed. We chatted camping fashion for a few minutes before taking seats with our lunch. I was two for two in the game of personal apologies! I was more at ease, my stomach felt more settled than it had in days, and I didn't have any tension behind my eyes.

Next up was Kevin Thomas, another costar in *The Wiz*.

I had said he was super stiff as Tinman—like, stiff-like-my-dead-grandfather stiff. I found him by the drinks station and walked up to him.

"June Motormouth Jackson," he said. "Got something else to say?"

"I deserve that," I responded. "I'm just here to say I'm sorry. Again."

"Why should I accept your apology?" he said, looking displeased.

My face fell as I tried to come up with a good reason. I'd insulted his dance moves and his acting ability. Maybe he would never try out for another school play because he'd been hurt by what I said. Maybe I'd ended the career of another great Black male lead because I made fun of him and killed his hopes and dreams. I was truly the worst person in the world. I wouldn't forgive me, either. I started to walk away.

"A'ight, June, whatever," he called after me.

I whipped around. "Whatever?"

"Yeah, like, whatever. Apology accepted or whatever."

I felt like I had to keep talking so that he'd have to listen to my apology and really feel that I meant it. "I'm really sorry, Kevin, I feel really, really horrible about what I said, and, like, you're a really great actor and you should totally keep acting!"

"Girl, I get it!" he said, frustrated. "You're sorry. A'ight.

I'm still going to call you Motormouth. Because you do run your mouth too much."

I thought that was a fair trade. "Okay, Kevin."

"Motormouth."

"Yes, I am," I said. "Thanks."

I looked around the room at the sixth-grade class and thought maybe there was hope for my future at Featherstone Creek. I got lost in a daydream, thinking about how my life post-leak and post-apology could improve. Then I saw a woman standing at the side of the room by herself, smiling at me. Giving me a thumbs-up. It was my chaperone—no, wait, that  hair, that smile . . . That was . . . of course . . .

"June!" I heard Olive call out. "Over here!"

I shook the daydream from my head and walked toward Olive. I looked back to that same corner of the room for my chaperone, or Victoria, or any woman. No one was standing there after all.

✦

Dear Journal,

My apology tour seems to be going well. I started at lunch and approached as many people as I could. Carmen accepted, as did Stacey Blackstone. Jermaine Hill teased me about looking like a <u>Stranger Things</u> cast member in my flannel shirt and Converse while fishing, but he accepted my apology. Kenya Barrett told me I shouldn't be allowed to have internet access after what I'd done. I didn't argue. She eventually shared her trail mix with me.

I apologized to Natalie Cross and Eustice Parker when I saw them at the cooking class, while we learned to cook a basic meal over a fire. A risk, but I did it. No one threw hot grits at me.

There are a few people I still need to apologize to, but I'm making good progress. Only one more night left. And then I can be free of this blessed spell. Free of Victoria. Free of having someone watching my every move. Listening to my every word! I can actually say what I want to say again! Like, I can express my feelings—good, bad, true, not so true. . . . OMG, can I lie again? Can I go back to my old ways of just saying what people want to hear so I don't have to worry about exposing my feelings again? There's no way

Victoria would let that happen, right? And I can't say
that behavior ever got me anywhere. Sigh . . .

It was right before dinner when I noticed that a bunch of
kids on the newspaper staff were sitting around the fire,
debating something of interest. I went over to the group,
curious. Quincy was talking fast.

"I think I've cracked it," he said. "It's something about
how the founders of Featherstone Creek aren't who everyone thinks they are."

"What do you mean?" Rachelle asked.

"No, like, I feel like in the papers, the story is always
how Featherstone Creek was founded by former slaves
who'd earned their freedom. Then they founded the town
and its businesses and bought the land with the money
they earned. Generations later, that's still the story. But
that's not how it actually went down."

I sat down next to Quincy. "How can you prove it?" I
asked.

"Well, you know old Sam LeSalle? The guy who used
to run the music store in town? He was willing to talk to
me and say it on the record."

My cheeks felt warm. "But one personal opinion isn't

enough, right?" I asked. "Do we have records? Deeds to homes? Any sort of historical documents?"

"Not right now," he said. "But maybe he can tell me where to get them."

I started to shift in my seat. Ms. West walked up behind Quincy and stood over us. "What's going on?" she asked.

Quincy explained his findings so far to Ms. West, who looked both entertained and impressed. As I listened to him retell the story, I felt a pang of jealousy and fear. I wished I had been the one to announce the latest scoop on the story. I wished I had juicy details to spill and could impress Ms. West and be that much closer to getting a front-page story in the newspaper. But I was also nervous about finding out the truth—my family's history was interwoven with the town's history. What if the secret involved my own family? I bit my lip and, for my own selfish reasons, hoped that ol' Sam LeSalle might change his mind and not say anything to Quincy. Maybe he'd talk to me instead. Or better yet, talk to no one and let sleeping secrets lie.

CHAPTER ELEVEN

$\blacklozenge\,\blacklozenge$
$\blacklozenge$

After the unofficial newspaper meeting and our last dinner at the main lodge, I wanted some time alone to think. I started to get that tension headache, the one that feels like a football player is sticking his thumbs into my temples and pressing them in like buttons on the sides of a pinball machine. I thought about Quincy's story, about the real story of Featherstone Creek. About my family story of Featherstone Creek.

Featherstone Creek was a well-respected historically Black town known for its enterprising, wealthy Black residents. My mom had been born and raised here, like her mother and her mother's mother and their families. They owned a fair share of land; at least, I had assumed as much, because when we were driving around town,

Mom always referred to certain businesses or houses as "ours" or "the family's": the medical center where Mom and her father had their practices, the mini storage off the main avenue. She was proud of our roots in this town. I sometimes heard Mom and Dad discussing what should be done with portions of the family land from time to time. Selling it was out of the question. Mom always gave the same answer whenever anyone asked her about selling: "June will decide one day."

When I was younger, I had no idea what that meant: "June will decide." So what, the fate of Featherstone Creek would fall to me? There was no way. I wouldn't sell it or move or give it up to anyone. I planned on living in this town my whole life. Even if I wanted to be some big Hollywood actress, I would still live here, or at least close by in Atlanta.

I stayed deep in my own head as I walked toward the cabin, wondering what Quincy knew, what he would find out about my family, if I'd have to say anything. Knowing that my family was one of the founding families, could I still report on the story? Ms. West had told us about bias in journalism during one of our meetings—bias was when the writer had a personal opinion on the story. Good reporters weren't supposed to have personal opinions in their writing. At least they weren't supposed to let their opinions affect their work. If I felt that my family was going to be hurt by the story, would I be biased? I had to think about—

SMACK.

I had run right into someone. "Oh man, I didn't see you—" I started to say, but stopped as soon as I saw the person's face. I blinked hard, trying to will away the vision I saw before me. Maybe she was a dream, or Victoria had shape-shifted? Nope. It was Nia standing there, looking as shocked as I felt.

"Hey," she said. "Sorry."

"No worries," I said, pretending not to be bothered by plowing face-first into my current worst frenemy.

Nia wanted to make sure I felt her presence, though. "I'm sorry," she said again. "I really didn't see you."

"No problem," I said, already walking away from her.

"Where are you going?" she asked, as if she cared. As if she hadn't ruined my life by exposing my blog to the entire world. As if I wasn't still mad at her. As if she wasn't still mad at me. I tried to respond as politely as I could.

"Back to my cabin. Gonna start getting ready for bed."

That was pleasant, not vengeful. But I was full of venge. Was she really going to just stand there and not say anything about the blog? *Again?*

I couldn't hold it in anymore. My brain had no more space for feelings—worry, anger, anything. I had to release some of them. I also needed this spell to end once and for all, and a huge step was to apologize to the person I'd hurt most, and who'd hurt me most in return. And here we were, face to face, with nothing between us but a few dragonflies and some crabgrass. My mouth opened, and I finally said what I'd wanted to say for weeks now:

"Nia, how could you do that to me?"

My voice quavered. Looking at her looking at me made a big lump grow in my throat. I'd thought that once I actually had this exchange with Nia, I would be so angry that I would call her every name in the book. But I couldn't get one more word out of my throat.

She looked away from me. Did she actually feel shame? I tried to clear my throat. Silence hung between us. It felt like a half hour had passed by.

"I'm sorry," Nia said.

"You're sorry?" *Wait, that's my line! I'm supposed to be apologizing to her!*

"I was just so angry and jealous of you," Nia said. "Everything for you seemed to be so perfect. And I was annoyed. Annoyed at your field hockey MVP status. Annoyed at your fancy new friend, Blake. Annoyed you got the lead in the school play . . ."

"You don't even like theater!" I exclaimed.

"Doesn't mean I wouldn't like it if I knew I could get the lead in the school play," Nia said. "And then when I found out you didn't tell me that Lee wanted to hang out with me . . . I knew you had the blog, and I thought you would be writing about your secret crush on Lee. I didn't know you had written all that nasty stuff about anyone else. When I read all that, I just lost it."

I listened, my stomach tying itself into knots as she spoke. I thought quickly about what I might have done in her position. Would I have done the same thing if I'd found out that my best friend was holding back on my crush and talking trash about the entire school? Probably.

There was much to unpack, but I chose my words slowly. "I didn't try to keep Lee from you," I said. "I just didn't want to lose my two closest friends at the same time. I was wrong for that, and I'm sorry. It was stupid."

Nia and I stared at each other for a second. I couldn't believe this moment was happening and we hadn't come to blows. Nia truly looked sad that she had hurt me. She looked like she had been hurting for a while, feeling like I was pulling away from her.

"Listen," I said, "I wrote some really bad things in that

blog about you and about everyone else, and I'm sorry. I shouldn't have done that."

"Yeah, you did," she said flatly. "But I'm not gonna say that some of that stuff about me wasn't true. I can be petty. I definitely don't like the outdoors. This whole camping thing is not my bag. I'm only here because my momma made me go." We both laughed at her confession.

"You don't know how hard it is to only be able to tell the truth to everyone," I said. "I don't want to hurt people's feelings and tell them things they don't want to hear. Like that they can't dance or I don't like the way they

sing. I can't even tell someone I like apples if I don't like apples. And I didn't want everyone to know my deepest secrets, like about Lee or that I'm insecure about my math skills. So I started the blog to keep the stuff I wouldn't tell anyone else in a place no one would ever see! Until you leaked it."

"Well, I'm sorry I leaked your private thoughts," Nia said. "Lots of people have a secret place where they write down what they really think. Maybe not everybody is as mean as you are, though. In my diary, I write my super-supersecret celebrity crushes. Like, super-duper secret. Like, I can't even tell you some of the people that are in there. But, dang, girl, you were, like, super mean to some people!"

"I knowwwww," I said, hanging my head. "Again, stupid and wrong. I wish I'd just written about my feelings for Lee in that blog. Instead, I made enemies of everyone."

"People were definitely angry at you," Nia said, nodding. "I mean, some of the things in there shocked me. But now people are over it. Or getting over it."

"Ugh," I said, and cringed. "I'm sorry. Nia, you're my best friend, and I shouldn't have written those things about you."

"I'm sorry, too, June," she said. "You're my best friend, and I'm sorry I leaked your private writing like that. That was super wrong."

"Well, I shut down the blog already, so we don't have to worry about any of this happening again. Let's just leave it in our past."

Nia nodded. "I'm down."

I looked at her and felt a connection again. Like she understood me. Suddenly the sun peeked through the dark clouds, and birds started to chirp. A rainbow appeared across the sky, and we grabbed hands and twirled under the large oak trees and sang "Kumbaya."

Okay, none of that happened.

But at least the anger in my belly started to ease up, and I was talking to my best friend again. Better than I could have imagined.

"So is that fairy godmother still following you around?" Nia asked.

"Yep, she's probably watching our exchange now and twirling around in her fairy dust."

Nia chuckled. "Is there any way to end the spell?"

"She told me I had to apologize to everybody here. Personally. Even after I wrote that column in the paper."

"I read that," Nia said. "The column was good. I stopped being as angry with you after I read it." Nia gave me a sympathetic look. "But now you can officially cross me off your apology checklist. We're good."

"Thanks," I said. We gave each other a fist bump and smiled.

On Monday morning we packed up our things and filed back onto the buses. My stomach felt way better than it had when I'd boarded the bus to come to Lake Lanier. But I still hadn't apologized to Lee, the second most important person—maybe even *more* important than Nia—that I needed to apologize to. The very last person on my list.

"Lee, wait up," I said as he was about to walk farther back on the bus. "Can you sit here for a second?"

Lee took a seat, slumping back to lean away from me. He clearly wanted to follow Alvin to another row of seats instead of dealing with me at that moment. But as if he had his grandmother's voice in his ear, telling him to sit up straight in front of a lady, he shimmied himself upright and turned his head. "W'sup?"

"I'm, um, I'm sorry. I really wanted you to know that. I was dumb."

Lee shook his head. He knew exactly what I was talking about, even though I hadn't mentioned the blog or Nia or any of it. "What you did was mad uncool, June."

"I know, and I feel horrible. And I was jealous and stupid, and I'm sorry."

Lee looked down and started picking at the seam of

his seat. Another day seemed to pass while I watched him continue to pick at a stray thread. "I don't know."

My heart broke. He was hurt. I had hurt him. I was doomed. I'd lied to him. I'd kept him from Nia. I'd done the one thing a best friend should not do. And he wouldn't forgive me. *Let me off this bus . . . let me . . .*

Lee looked up from the seat. "I'll forgive you if you do one thing for me."

Anything! I'll beg! Plead! Wear a sign that says I'm the worst friend ever! "Sure."

"You have to babysit Chadwick on Tuesdays when I have Creeks club meetings."

What? How was I supposed to babysit a pet lizard?

"You sing to him, play with him, just keep him company. He's getting lonely during the days, and I need someone to be with him. My grandma can't do it—she's allergic to his skin or something, so she says. And Chadwick really likes you. Now that field hockey's over, you've got some time, right?"

What the . . . ? I was supposed to go to his house and sing to his pet lizard? This is how I had to earn back his friendship? Chadwick was going to make or break our relationship? Oh boy. I sighed. I knew if I wanted to save our friendship, I needed to spend some quality time with that reptile.

"Deal," I said. "But I'm not going to hold him in my coat pocket or anything. I'll talk to him through his cage."

Lee grumbled. "But he needs skin-to-skin contact!"

I imagined holding Chadwick up to my cheek to . . . snuggle . . . him. I shivered in my seat at the thought. "Really?"

Lee relented. "Ugh, fine, just keep an eye on him."

"Okay," I agreed. We shook hands.

"Fine," Lee said. "I forgive you, then."

A wave of relief washed over me. Lee's apology was the biggest one I'd had to make. Earning the forgiveness of the person at the center of my leaked-blog drama would convince Victoria to lift the spell, right? I looked around for fairy dust or haze or glitter. Anything. Was she watching? Victoria was on this bus, right? Even if she wasn't on this bus, I knew she had to be witnessing this breakthrough from somewhere nearby.

At the very least, knowing that Lee had forgiven me lifted my spirit. He was one of my oldest friends, and not having his *true* friendship—not just the polite kind— would have left something missing in my life. I'd now apologized to my closest friends: Lee, Nia, and Olive. Heck, once Victoria lifted the spell and this blog drama was officially behind me, maybe I could actually thrive socially in my next few years at FCMS.

I leaned back in my seat next to Lee. The tension in my shoulders relaxed, and my neck muscles loosened. Lee looked down at his shoes, and I turned my head toward the window for a bit, too nervous to see his reaction now that we'd cleared the air. Something had changed between us. A wall had come down with the apology, and it was as if two friends who had been far away from each other for some time were finally coming together again. Not a running-into-each-other's-arms kind of reunion, but like a "nice to see you again" type of thing.

It was nice to sit next to Lee again.

I turned back toward him. He stopped fidgeting with his shoe and pulled out something from his bookbag. "You want a granola bar? Saved a few from the lodge."

"Thanks," I said. I'd never been more grateful for a snack than I was on that bus ride home with my old friend.

CHAPTER TWELVE

✦ ✦
✦

By the time I finally arrived home Monday afternoon, I was spent. I needed a proper shower. I still had dirt under my fingernails from the Sunday-morning fishing trip. I smelled like bug spray and burning wood. My parents were eager to hear all the details and cooked a barbecue dinner to celebrate my return. School was out for the rest of the week for our spring break—and I was definitely going to take that time to recover from our trip.

While they got dinner ready, I took one of the longest showers I'd ever taken, letting the hot water burn off any speck of dirt left on me and completing an extended hair wash, conditioning, and hair mask before I stepped out of the steaming bathroom. My robe had never felt so plush and so luxurious. I was thankful to be back in my room, alone and wrapped in fabrics that weren't fireproof.

My mind started to drift to the story about Featherstone Creek. Should I ask my mom about it? Maybe she had some inside scoop. Like, better inside scoop than Quincy's gossip from what's-his-name from the car wash. I put on leggings and an oversized T-shirt and went downstairs.

The weather was warm enough for just a light jacket. Dad had fired up the grill and was cooking away outside. I could smell the barbecue chicken from inside the kitchen, which reminded me of the campfires I'd just left behind. Mom had made a string bean casserole and served ice cream for dessert. It was as if the whole dinner was an ode to my camping trip. But it definitely tasted better than the food at the camp.

We sat at our kitchen table, and I told my parents about the weekend. The apologies. Nia. The rumor about Left-Eye Louie. "Have you ever heard about that?" I asked.

"No," Mom said. "Never ever. But he sounds super scary. Did you all see him?"

"No!" I said. "Well, I don't think so."

I looked at my mom as I watched her eat. It seemed like now was a good time to ask about the newspaper story. "There is something interesting that did come up on the trip. I told you about those rumors about the founding families of Featherstone Creek . . . ?"

"What rumors?"

I swallowed hard. "People are saying that, like, basically the founders of this town aren't who they say they are," I said. "Someone discovered documents or, like, evidence to prove it, and I think we're getting closer to publishing a story. We just have to talk to a few more people."

Mom and Dad started looking super uncomfortable, like I had picked my nose at the dinner table. Mom pressed her lips together softly and looked at me. "June, dear. Oh boy, okay, there is something I should discuss with you."

I felt the mood change at the table. It suddenly felt colder inside than it was outside. Was there some big family secret I didn't know about that was going to embarrass me? Was this going to leave me with absolutely no friends at school? Had I just gone on an embarrassing apology tour to regain trust from the FCMS student body for nothing?

"I was waiting until you were older to tell you this, but I guess now is as good a time as any. You should know the real story of how Featherstone Creek was founded."

Oh snap! There *was* a secret! And my mother knew it! My stomach dropped. I was scared. And strangely excited! Could it really be my luck that I was going to crack the biggest secret of Featherstone Creek by interviewing my own mother? No one was going to have a firsthand source as good as mine!

"Okay, I'm listening," I said. "Wait! Should I get my notebook? I should write all of this down!"

"Hold on," my mother said nervously. "Just listen first."

I leaned in closer. Mom took a deep breath. "So, as you know, this town is and has been proudly African American–founded and African American–owned. But the one thing that people don't talk about much in its history is that the initial investment to start Featherstone Creek came from a white man."

I sat there for a second, still as a snail on a twig. That was a tidbit I had not been expecting. There were white people in Featherstone Creek who had been here awhile, but none of them were founding families. And the town had been founded during the 1800s, when slavery still existed. I thought very few white men would be interested in giving a Black man or woman funds to incorporate their own town during that time. I could not imagine what Southern white man would be one of the founders of one of the most affluent Black suburbs in Georgia.

My mother sat back in her seat for a minute and then continued. "So back back back in the day, as you know, one of my great-great-great-grandparents was one of the original founders of Featherstone Creek. My great-great-great-grandmother was a freed slave and stumbled upon this area along with other freed slaves. They were some of the first people to arrive and settle on the land. So the land was theirs. But what they needed was money to build.

"Although I've shown you pictures of your great-great-great-great-grandparents, I don't think I ever showed you a picture of your real great-great-great-great-grandfather. He died young, but he founded Featherstone Creek with your grandmother before he passed away."

Mom got up from the table to head to the den to look for something. I looked at Dad, wondering if he'd known all of this before. "Did you have any idea about this?"

"Some, but not the details," he said. "I'm taking notes, just like you."

Mom returned to the kitchen. I had questions. "Okay, so my great-great-great-great-grandparents founded Featherstone Creek. With a loan from a white guy. Okay, that's, like, interesting. But where is the scandal? Where's the intrigue?"

Mom looked down. Dad nodded approvingly. "Oh-kay, supersleuth!" he said. "You're like that guy from *Dateline* trying to dig up unsolved mysteries. These are great skills for Howard, you know."

To my dad, *any* skill is a great skill for Howard.

"It's . . . complicated . . . ," my mother said.

She pushed our dinner plates aside and placed an old wooden box on the table. She opened it and rifled through a few photos, news clippings, and other documents. Then she pulled out a photo. It was gray and tattered along the

sides, but I could see two people standing together in the image. One was my great-great-great-great-grandmother looking straight ahead; the other was a white man standing next to her.

"Who is this man?" I asked.

"That's your great-great-great-great-grandfather. And he, along with your grandmother and a few others, founded Featherstone Creek."

I looked at the photo, puzzled. I had heard stories about my great-great-great-great-grandmother. I knew that she had done some big things to help develop Featherstone Creek, but I had no idea that she'd founded the town with somebody else. Nor did I know that that somebody else was a white man.

"You mean to tell me that one of the founders of Featherstone Creek was a white man, and that white man was my great-great-great-great-grandfather?"

My mother pressed her lips together. "I know, June. I know you have a lot of questions. There's a lot of things that I waited a long time to tell you. But, yes, that is the truth."

My mother sat up in her seat and cleared her throat.

"Listen, June, back then it was illegal for them to be married. Your great-great-great-great-grandmother was a freed slave, your great-great-great-great-grandfather was a white man who owned land but was against slavery. He met your grandmother and they fell in love. But to be together, they had to run away from their lives, from the towns they knew and that knew them, to start a new life. To be safe."

I felt a headache coming on—processing all this new information was a lot of work.

My mother continued. "They found an open parcel of land and settled there. They grew crops, sent word to their friends and families, and they too came and settled here. They were happy and got things up and running quite quickly, but after a few years, your great-great-great-great-grandfather fell ill and passed away."

I felt like I was listening to a slavery-era drama starring Viola Davis as the lead, not my family history. "Before he died, he left his deed and rights to the town to my triple-great-grandmother, and they made a pact that their part of Featherstone Creek would always stay in the family. Over the years, your ancestors left parcels to the women in their families and helped people found businesses here. As time passed, the story of your great-great-great-great-grandfather's involvement fell out of the family history. Some thought it was better that people believed Featherstone Creek was completely Black-founded and Black-owned. It kept things . . . neater."

I was stunned. I never knew anything of Featherstone Creek's history except that it had been founded as a strong Black town. I'd never even thought much about my ancestors. I'd just always assumed we were one of the Black families who had settled here, and that we took it upon ourselves to educate ourselves and to create businesses to serve our families. I knew about slavery. I had assumed some of our family members had once been enslaved. I knew about Jim Crow and civil rights, but I had never heard this history-changing story about my own family.

But *why* hadn't I heard it before?

Did my family not want it known that the town had been cofounded by a white man? Were they the ones going around forbidding people to talk about the truth? Did they cancel people left and right who knew this information? OMG, was my family covering up the truth?!

But if people knew the truth, wouldn't they see that at the heart of this story was true love? Two people— my great-great-great-great-grandparents—trying to fight a system that didn't allow them to be in love? How could this be seen as a bad thing? Or a big secret? This was a secret that could show the real truth behind Feather-stone Creek's founding. That it was part of a forbidden love story that endured despite the deplorable practice of slavery at the time. Wouldn't people feel inspired by that?

I wanted to tell people about our family history, how pioneering my ancestors were to found our town. But why had Mom been so secretive?

"I want to tell everyone about this," I said. "Why hasn't anyone told the truth?"

My mom cleared her throat. "Well, because I think some people were ashamed. Ashamed about how people might feel about the truth, about a white man being responsible for founding the town. About our involvement.

I think some family members just thought it was easier to say nothing."

"But, Mom," I said, thinking back to what I had heard during the camping trip, "people have been looking into the story for years. For our school paper and other papers. But they've been blocked every time someone asks questions. People have been unwilling to talk. Have we basically forbidden everyone to talk about this?"

"Well, *forbid* is a strong word," Mom said defensively.

"Well, that's what it feels like."

Mom wriggled uncomfortably in her seat and leaned toward me. "June, I'm not the only one who has an opinion about his. Your elders, my elders, have also had their feelings, and I did my best to respect them."

My father finally chimed in. "Yeah, but, honey, it is a major secret no one wanted to admit. June's right— people got shut down anytime someone wanted to share the truth."

"It was respecting the elders' wishes," my mom said to him sharply.

"Things have changed, honey," Dad said. "Everyone wants the truth about everything these days, even if it hurts. Authenticity."

My mom looked down at the pictures. I looked at my dad. I agreed with him. It was time for the truth to be told about Featherstone Creek. And it was time that we as a family took hold of that truth. And that I, reporter for the *Featherstone Post*, shared that truth with the public. After all—I was Honest June. It was my job to tell the truth.

"So, about this article, Mama," I asked quietly. "We should tell this story. This is your story as much as it is mine. It's a beautiful love story, and my great-great-great-great-grandfather did a lot to establish this town and create a safe place for his family—and others, too."

Mom leaned back. I could tell she wasn't immediately convinced she should let the truth out. "June, telling this story is a big responsibility. I hope you think hard about this. It could impact many families here. It could become national news. You'd have to write it in a way that's respectful, that doesn't hurt people. Because some are still scared."

I didn't want to hurt anyone. I was proud of our family! And I wanted to share the truth with everyone. And, okay, I knew this was selfish, but I wanted a scoop on the front page of the paper! "Are you saying I can't write it?"

"No," Mom said.

"Okay, then! To write it, I need you to tell me everything and go on the record. Will you help me?"

"I . . . ," she started to say.

"Been long enough, honey," my dad said, turning to her.

My mom nodded. "Okay."

My head throbbed. The wheels inside were turning so hard, so fast. My mother looked worried—worried about the reaction to the truth, worried about my next move.

My dad shrugged. "Y'all could have a big story on your hands."

My mind suddenly took off like a rocket. I had to write this down. I had to gather research, all of the photos, old wills, old land deeds! I jumped out of my seat. "I gotta get my notebook and laptop. May I go to my room?"

"Of course," Mom said.

"Don't blast it on social media just yet!" Dad said. "I know how you kids are."

"Dad, trust me: I don't blast anything online anymore after the blog incident," I said.

I stood up and hurried toward my room, taking the steps two at a time with big leaps. I ran through the long

hallway, past several family photos of Mom, Dad, my grandparents, and our family gatherings. I took a breath and looked at those photos, wondering if everyone in the photos knew what I knew. My entire family history had been rewritten over dinner. There was so much to digest, in more ways than one.

CHAPTER THIRTEEN

✦✦
✦

After dinner, I opened the door to my room and flopped onto my bed. The gears in my brain were spinning at full speed, so fast I could have sworn I saw smoke come out of my ears when I walked past the mirror on my dresser. I needed to talk this through with someone. Chloe!

> **JUNE: Girl. Girl! We. Need. To. Talk!**

I sat in front of my computer and immediately fired up Google. I searched for "Featherstone Creek." My family. My grandparents. I saw old photos of old buildings and old businesses, old newspaper articles with historical events and news announcements. I saw many large groups of dark-skinned families, many with the last names of kids I went to school with. But nowhere did I see a random white guy on a horse or with a woman who looked like my great-great-great-great-grandmother or anyone else in my family lineage. My eyes darted back and forth across the screen. Was it all true? And was it true that no one had ever revealed the truth until now?

Chloe finally FaceTimed me. "I'm putting on a hair mask," she said when I answered. "What's up? How was the camping trip? Did you survive?"

"I'll tell you later," I said. "It was fine. I survived. But Mom just told me the biggest news I've ever heard. There's a big story everyone's been looking into about the real founders of Featherstone Creek. Turns out my family is behind it all."

"What do you mean?" Chloe said. She didn't sound as surprised as I was. I'd expected more shock and awe. I was getting an unbothered vibe.

I went into everything. I explained about my great-great-great-great-gran, about my white great-great-great-great-gramps. About the love story, the deed, the promise to keep Featherstone Creek Black-owned. Black female–owned. Chloe shrugged.

"Wow," she said, barely interested.

"Wow?" I said. Was I on mute? Did she not hear the details that I just unleashed during this phone call? "That's all you got for me?"

"I mean . . . ," Chloe said, looking off to the side. "I mean, how can I say this without you getting mad at me. . . . We kinda knew this."

I almost dropped the phone. Who was *we*? What did *we* know? Her and Nia? Her family? Now my head was about to explode. "How could my best friend know this and not tell me?" I exclaimed.

"I heard my parents talking about it a long time ago, and I assumed you didn't know, so I didn't say anything," she said. Her shoulders had risen up to her ears. "I also didn't know how true it was because they were talking about it like it was just a rumor, so I didn't want to spread lies. It's an awesome story, though! So much love and your great-grandparents were such pioneers! You should be really proud."

I was still shocked that Chloe knew this before I did. "But you heard me say I was looking into this big scoop for the paper! Why didn't you tell me then?"

"I didn't know this was that big scoop! I forgot about it until you just told me right now!"

I felt a ringing in my ears. How in the world did someone who lived so far, all the way in California, know the history of Featherstone Creek better than I did? Me, who lived in the actual town and whose mother's ancestor had founded it? I felt like my own history was getting away from me.

"Who else knows about this?" I said. "Seems no one in Featherstone Creek knows."

"Have you asked?"

"What do you mean, have I asked? Who would I ask? Does Nia know?"

Chloe bit her lip. I could tell from her nervous look what the answer was. "She told me she heard her father talking about it one day."

Does no one tell me anything anymore?

"You all weren't speaking for, like, a month, June!"

I couldn't breathe. This reminded me of those family sitcoms where the parents are breaking up and the kids are the last to know. If it weren't for this newspaper article that had everyone looking into the story, when would I have found out about my family? Would everyone but me have known this secret?

I hung up on Chloe, mad. Not mad at her for not telling me, but mad at my family for trying to keep me in the dark.

I texted Nia:

> **JUNE:** How long have you known
> that my great-great-great-great-
> grandfather was white? And a founder
> of Featherstone Creek??

Honestly, I preferred no response. I didn't want to know that Nia had been keeping this from me. And if she knew, who had she told? Was she planning to expose this secret just like she'd exposed my secret blog?

Surprisingly, Nia answered right away.

> **NIA:** I heard my parents talking about
> it one night. I didn't know it was
> actually true.

I was speechless. I was literally the last person in Featherstone Creek to know the truth about my own family.

> **NIA:** Your mom has tried to block
> this story from coming out for years.
> Seems she's finally had a change of
> heart. My mom and dad always said it
> should be shared.

NIA: I'm sorry I kept it from you. It just was not my truth to tell.

I was surprised she had held such huge, life-changing information to herself. I thought about that comment, "not my truth to tell." She was right. It was my story to tell.

And I was going to be the one who told it.

Dear Journal,

Everyone knew my great-great-great-great-grandfather was white—except for me? Okay, at least maybe everyone had heard this rumor before, except for me? Why the heck did my parents keep this from me? It's, like, the greatest love story of all time—a man and a woman who legally can't be together but who find a way to overcome the odds to not only be together but create a place where they and their families can live safely? That's, like, Nobel Prize–level stuff! What a great story!

A story . . . that I finally get to tell the whole town in the school paper.

CHAPTER FOURTEEN

✦✦
✦

For the first time in a long time, I actually looked forward to school. I looked forward to talking with other people and having them hear what I had to say. For weeks, no one cared about what I had to say because what I had to say wasn't that nice. But I finally felt at peace—I had made my amends on the camping trip. I had my friends back. And now I had a responsibility to change history. For the better.

✦

I spent the rest of my spring break doing research on our town and gathering my notes about my findings to present to Ms. West. On Monday, our first day back in school since break, I tracked down Ms. West before classes started. I walked quickly to the newspaper lab and spotted her in the back, organizing books. "Ms. West, I figured out the story."

"Really?" Ms. West said. "The Featherstone Creek story? How? What do you mean?"

I dove right into the details. I told her everything about everything—the surprise cofounder of Featherstone Creek, that he was a member of my own family, and that he had helped create the town as a safe haven, out of love for my great-great-great-great-grandmother. I told Ms. West that I had a first-person account of the

details from a direct descendant. My breath grew faster with every sentence. Sweat beaded on my upper lip.

Ms. West was breathless when I finished. After a moment of stunned silence, she spoke. "June, since you're the one who knows the truth, would you like to write a piece for the school paper about what you've learned?"

A flutter tickled my chest. My name attached to this story would be certain to cause controversy. But it was a truth people had wanted to know for a long time, a truth that could inspire others and bring a sense of pride they might not have known before. It could certainly bring that to my family if I did it right.

"I'd be honored," I said.

I walked into the hall with a pep in my step, with more confidence now that I knew I had the big scoop. Carmen gave me a nod as I walked to my locker. Nia and Olive smiled and waved when I walked into homeroom. I was still on cloud nine when lunchtime rolled around and I was set to join everyone at our usual table for lunch. Nia was already sitting there and watched me as I came to the table. "So, any gossip from the camping trip?" she asked.

I had gossip for sure, but restraint had served me well

in these post-blog times. I stayed quiet and let the rest of the group start.

"I heard that when we did that trust exercise where we had to fall, people dropped Darnell Woods on his back and he bruised his tailbone," Lee said.

"Whoa, word?" Alvin asked. "I didn't hear that, but is that why he was walking weird on Saturday? He seemed fine on the bus ride home."

"Rachelle thought she got bedbugs from her bed," Olive said. "She showed me her arm and thought she had bumps all over it. I told her I thought it was just dry skin and to put some baby oil on it. Worked like magic. She texted me today to say they're gone."

"Good," I said. "'Cause if *she* had bedbugs, then we would *all* have bedbugs!"

"I mean, the sheets were a little itchy," Lee said. "Knew I shoulda brought a sleeping bag."

"What about the assignments? Did everyone finish theirs? Are we getting graded on them?" Alvin said.

"I don't know. At the staff meeting before school this morning, the principal said she was proud of everyone's work, apparently," Olive said.

I thought back to our camping trip. I remembered how Alvin had made a fishing pole out of a stick and some twine during our fishing assignment ("I like building things from scratch," he'd said) and had perfectly pitched a tent with his group during our Setting Up Camp workshop. "You did awesome, Alvin," I assured him.

"Your camping wasn't too bad, June," Alvin responded, twiddling his thumbs. "You'd survive in the woods if you needed to."

My cheeks started to grow hot. "Thanks," I said softly. How in the world could things get any more awkward between us? How had we gone from shining stars in the school play together to two totally awkward humans who couldn't even sit at lunch without fumbling over each other's words?

Our chatter seemed to change course quickly. Lee suddenly turned toward the vending machines. "I need some snacks for later. I'll be back," he declared, then got up from the table and scooted off.

Olive and Blake became engrossed in conversation about orchestra, and Nia started chatting over her shoulder with another girl. Alvin and I turned toward each other. I looked at him shyly.

I realized he was the one person I hadn't yet apologized to for the horrible things I'd said online. He'd been kind to me on the entire trip, even confessing to me that he liked hanging out with me. I was so caught up in the glee of him thinking I was cool—and the embarrassment of me saying "right back atcha" in response—that I'd forgotten about the sting he must've felt over my comments

about him on the blog. Now was my time to clear the air. I gathered up the smallest bit of courage left in my soul.

"Hey, um, I need to tell you something," I said. Alvin looked down at his hands. "I'm sorry."

"Sorry about what?" he said. "You just said I was good at camping."

"No, not that," I said. "I'm sorry about what I said about you on my blog. I feel horrible, because I actually think you're, like, cool."

"Yeah?" Alvin said, looking right at me. It was all of a sudden quite warm in the cafeteria. My hands were getting sweaty.

"You can code, you can sing, and you can camp," I said. I leaned into what I thought was true about Alvin, my best effort to cancel out calling him a computer nerd on the blog. "Really, is there anything you don't know how to do?"

"I can't do a backflip," he said. "I tried at the pool a bunch last year. Still can't get it."

"You can practice on my trampoline anytime," I said. My cheeks were warm and red. The expression on my face made it clear that I thought Alvin was one of the coolest guys I knew. But more important, I wanted him to know how I truly felt so we could both forget what I'd said about him on that dumb blog. "Anyway, I hope you can forgive me."

Alvin gave a quick chuckle and looked away. "I'd forgotten you'd even talked about me on your blog until you said something," he said.

"Oh, good . . . then, um, can we keep forgetting about it, then?" I said, sitting up a little taller.

"Okay," Alvin said.

"Deal." I smiled. I heard birds chirping in my ears. I couldn't hide my mix of relief, happiness, and anxiousness over what could happen now that I'd apologized. I tried to straighten my expression.

"You serious about that trampoline thing?" he said to me.

I felt my stomach flip-flop at those words. "Of course! Why not? I'm on it all the time!" I laughed nervously. He smiled, grateful for the invitation. It wouldn't be the first time he'd come over to my house, but something in my gut told me things would be different, maybe even more fun, when he came over in the future.

"And, of course," I said, taking a deep breath to say what I should have said last week, "I like hanging out with you, too."

He stood up from the table just as Lee returned. "Right back atcha," he said, giving me a wink. I twisted my lips to hold in both my embarrassment and giddiness in front of my friends. Even though that phrase had made me cringe when I'd said it, somehow now it had a much better ring to it.

CHAPTER FIFTEEN

✦ ✦

S ince I'd met with Ms. West, I spent every
afternoon typing away at my computer, finishing
off my article. I had asked my mom if I could publish
a photo of my great-great-great-great-grandparents in
the newspaper, the best bit of evidence to prove my
grandfather's existence, and Mom gave me the picture
of him standing beside the horse. I was a bit nervous
about what the reaction might be to the photo of my
grandfather included with my article. Would people
think he was a hero? A fake? Either way, I needed all
the documents I could find to make my story as authentic as possible.

Ms. West had volunteered to read over the article a
few times before it was published, and to speak with my

mother to make sure she approved of what I'd written. (I wondered if the editors of the *New York Times* or the *Atlanta Journal-Constitution* had needed their mother's approval when they wrote their first newspaper stories in school?) All three of us reviewed deeds and documents that my mom had given us to support the story.

"This is going to be big," Ms. West said. "I wouldn't be surprised if Channel 5 called you for an interview."

"Wow, really?" I said. "We could be on television for this?"

My mother looked nervous. "I mean, we're not in this for the publicity," Mom told Ms. West. "But this is a historic moment. It's setting the record straight. If it helps educate people, then I'm all for it."

Finally, after a few days of preparation, we were ready to send the files for the latest issue of the school newspaper off to the printer—with my article on the front page. My mother reread the last version of the story in layout on Thursday night and, for the first time, she looked less worried. "This is a historic moment, June," she said. "Nobody's ever known this history, and I think you have written it in a respectful and informative way. Your ancestors would be proud."

I sat up a little taller in my seat. My truth about my family was about to be revealed to the *Featherstone Post*–reading public when the paper released on Monday. I felt surprisingly calm, despite knowing what could happen next. My mom seemed comfortable and smiled at me. I emailed Ms. West that we approved of the final article and the layout, and awaited her response.

Okay, June—off to the printer it goes. Congratulations on your big story.

Ms. West

I leaned back in my chair and relaxed as my mom hugged my shoulders from behind.

◆

I was anxious walking into school on Friday, knowing that my story was about to be on the front page of the school paper, which would be in everyone's hands soon. I had worked hard on the story and gotten the blessing of my mother, who had gotten the blessings of her living family members. Ms. West had approved the article. Even Quincy, who'd seen me working on the final drafts with Ms. West in the newspaper office, had told me he was excited to read the truth. "I want to see if homie from the car wash was right!"

I went to lunch to join the rest of my friends. I wasn't sure I would eat, but I definitely had some tea to spill.

"So, June, what's up at the paper lately? You should do a feature on *my* personal style," Nia teased.

"Actually, not a bad idea," I said. "But I have a bigger story that I'm about to crack. It involves my own family."

"Word?" Lee said, his eyes widening. "What did you guys do? Embezzlement? Tax evasion?"

"No, fool, it's none of those things," I said, sucking my teeth. "It's about who really founded Featherstone Creek."

Alvin put his spoon down. "It was founded by four founding families, Black families. Black-owned, Black-run."

"Not exactly," I said.

I went into the story, explaining everything about my great-great-great-great-grandfather and his skin color, about the deed of the town and how it had been transferred to his wife, then to their daughter, then to other women and eventually the modern descendants of the founding families. My friends' eyes grew wider and wider as I spoke. Nia looked over and remained quiet as my

voice carried the conversation for what seemed like a half hour but was really about two minutes.

There was a bit of silence when I finished. Then Lee spoke.

"I've been hearing about this for a while," he said. "Every time the rumors would pop up again, I heard my grandparents whispering about it. Or my grandmom would call your mom. So, yeah, it's a thing."

"Wait, so you knew? And you never said anything?" I asked.

"Well, I didn't exactly know what they were whispering about, but now that I put two and two together, the whispers always came when somebody was trying to, like, claim they knew the truth about Featherstone Creek. So I figured that's what they were talking about."

The more people I talked to about this story, the more I felt like a lot of them already knew it. Again, was I the last to know about the rumor?

"Anyway, I wrote about it for the *Post*. I wanted to give you all a heads-up, because the issue with my article is coming out on Monday. The truth. The real truth. About my family."

"Cool," Lee said. Everyone nodded in unison. "Were you scared to write the stuff about your own family? Must've been, like, heavy," he added.

I looked at him and shrugged. "A little. I'm not sure what people will think. But who else was going to tell it?"

The group nodded again.

"Well, I'm proud of you, girl," Nia said. "What are people going to say—it's the truth! And a good story. I can't wait to read it."

"Me too," said Olive.

"Me three," Alvin said.

"Thanks," I said. I nibbled on a bit of my sandwich, hoping that the reactions from the rest of the student body were just as warm.

Exclusive: Featherstone Creek's True Roots

FOR THE FIRST TIME EVER, THE REAL FOUNDERS OF FEATHERSTONE CREEK WILL BE REVEALED. BUT THEY MAY NOT BE WHO YOU THINK THEY ARE.

BY JUNE JACKSON

Featherstone Creek has prided itself on being "for us, by us." Founded by Black settlers just after the slavery era, the property has been kept in the hands of founding families for generations. But among the founding families was one Tyrone Hughes: a white man, and my great-great-great-great-grandfather. This is his story. Our story.

I didn't know anything about Tyrone Hughes until recently. I didn't hear any rumors about the real founders of Featherstone Creek until a few weeks ago. But once I asked my family about the chatter, they couldn't hide the truth anymore. They didn't want to.

Our ancestor, Tyrone Hughes, fell in love with my great-great-great-great-grandmother Belle during a time when it wasn't safe for a white man to be with a Black woman. He loved her so much that he wanted to create a safe place for them to live and raise a family. He found a plot of land and invited some close friends to join them. They did, and together the small group founded what we now know as our hometown: Featherstone Creek.

Not only did he love her so much that he created a town for her, but he put her name on their share of the land so that she would always be known as a cofounder of Featherstone Creek. Now, when the history books cover the roots of our town, they include the Black founders listed in official prop- erty and town records. But Tyrone's role in how Featherstone Creek came to be shouldn't be erased from history. Here's his story.

On Monday, a special edition of the *Featherstone Post* landed in the hallways with my story on the front page. It made a splash, such a splash that the principal gave a copy to a friend of hers at Atlanta's Channel 5 News. By lunch-time, Ms. West had gotten a call from a producer who im-mediately wanted to feature the story on the six o'clock news program. Ms. West called my mother and asked if the two of us would like to appear for an interview. Tele-vision! I thought I might end up on TV for my acting, but this was just as good!

My mom met me after school and we both reported to Ms. West's office to prepare for the interview. The news team decided to do the story at the school, and they set up cameras in a conference room. Someone came over to clip small microphones onto our clothes. Then an older man who wore a suit and had a geometrically perfect fade haircut asked me questions, like why I was interested in the history of Featherstone Creek and how long my mom had held it secret.

"My June is a very smart girl. I knew I couldn't keep the truth from her for too long," my mom said. "It's time the new generation of Featherstone Creek knows their real roots. And celebrates them. It's up to young people to carry the torch. And they can only do that by knowing the real history behind the town's founding."

After the school interview, the producers came to my house to get footage of the pictures we had of our family, some shots of the maps and artifacts we had uncovered, and other quotes from my mom. They said it would broadcast during the evening news. How they could produce this so fast was beyond me.

And as they promised, it was the first story they featured at six p.m. My parents and I sat down together with my grandmother. (Grandpa was still at his office—he called us afterward.) Grandma smiled and put her hand

on my shoulder. "It's a shock. Never thought I'd be around to see the day. But it's the truth."

"Are you afraid of what people might say?" I asked her.

"I'm too old to care what people think anymore," she said. "But it's the truth, so it doesn't matter what people think. You can't fight the truth."

Everyone in the sixth grade tuned in to watch the news report. I got a ton of texts, but not as many as I did after "the leak." The emails and notes continued to come in all evening.

For those who had missed the news show, Mrs. Worth rebroadcast it in homeroom on Tuesday. People were super interested in the story. Nia teased me as I walked into math the next morning: "Okay, Tamron Hall!" she cried out. I smiled as I sat down. No more secrets. No more lies.

CHAPTER SIXTEEN

✦ ✦
✦

Dad was so proud about my newspaper achievements that he wanted to take me out for dinner to celebrate. Mom had to work late at the hospital on Tuesday night, so we drove to the Crab Shack, just the two of us, and sat in our usual booth. I was starving from my hard work this week. "Order whatever you want," Dad said. "It's on me."

"It's always on you, Dad."

"I know, June," he said in a joking tone. "Dad jokes!"

We looked over the menu, though by now we knew what our favorites were. When the waitress came to take our order, I studied her face closely. She looked down at her notepad the entire time, not making much eye contact. She smiled as she grabbed our menus, but the oversized plastic folders blocked her face as she took them away. Maybe Sheila/Victoria had the night off?

Dad leaned in toward me. "So, wanted to talk to you about something," he said.

Oh no, here we go. Howard? Law school? Field hockey?

"Mom's been telling me you've been having some . . . issues?" Dad asked.

"Issues?" I asked. *Mom! What did you tell him?*

"Are you feeling stressed? Unhappy?" he asked.

Where was this Dr. Phil moment coming from? I thought we'd finally reached a good place, and now he was probing for problems?

"I'm not unhappy. I just had a front-page story in the *Post*! I was on actual television? Why would I be unhappy?"

"Well, you have a lot on your plate," Dad said. "And, you know, that blog leak thing was a big deal. You were pretty upset by that."

"I was," I said. "But I apologized and I wrote the column, and people forgave me, so . . . I'm good," I said. I *was* good. Right? And we were good, too. I had been honest and open with my dad in a way I'd thought was impossible a few months ago, before meeting Victoria. I had told him my true feelings about school, my grades, the pressure to make everyone happy, and he had also shared some big confessions about his own insecurities.

The truth had brought us closer. That definitely was a good thing.

The waitress delivered our plates and scooted away before I could get a look at her. Dad paused for a moment as if he was collecting his thoughts, and then cleared his throat.

"June, when I was growing up, eleven felt older than it is now. I knew a lot more about the world at eleven than I think you do. But I do think you kids these days have so much more to worry about. Social media. Social justice. Making changes in the world for a better future. You know I only want what's best for you. I've worked so hard. Your mother has worked so hard. And you know I had it tough growing up. My parents weren't wealthy like your mother's parents. I know what it feels like to have life be harder for you than it needs to be. So I just feel it's my obligation to prepare you for the real world."

"Dad, I watch the news!" I said. (Heck, I *was* the news the other day.) "I read a lot of things. I know what's fair and right. I know how I should be treated."

"How you should be treated?" Dad said.

"Well," I said, now sitting up in my chair. I felt my heart rate increase. "Like going to Atlanta and having that woman at that store racially profile me? That was just so rude. I was not going to take that." Did I just say that out loud? To my father? It was like I had this sudden burst of confidence and power. Superhero power. Like Victoria had meant when she described my truth-telling ability.

Dad nodded. "Ah, June. Mom told me about that one. We're so used to hearing or seeing that kind of ignorant behavior from people that I don't think either of us would have reacted like you did. And you were right to be upset."

Dad reached his hand over the table and put it on my forearm. I felt like we were two grown people having a grown-people conversation. Now I could see what Victoria had meant when she said the curse wasn't a curse at all; it was a blessing. A superpower.

Maybe now was the time to drop one more truth bomb on him, since I was on a roll. I had been thinking about my future as an actress and as a writer. I'd also been thinking about Howard. There was a way to combine them that I knew would make my dad beyond happy.

"Dad, I have a secret I want to share with you," I said. "When I was doing research on Featherstone Creek, I stumbled onto some archives on the Howard University website. I started digging around the website a bit, and I read there's a new drama department there. Maybe Howard *could* be my dream school. Just not Howard Law. But maybe I could check out that new Chadwick A. Boseman College of Fine Arts! I really see a future in the arts. I'm

not sure if it's singing or drama or writing. But I just like artsy stuff. That's my vibe," I said.

I held my breath. An uncomfortable silence hung over us. Maybe I'd gone too far. I knew Dad wanted me to follow the path of advanced degrees, law, medicine, business. But I felt this creative pull. He looked down at his food and took a slow bite. Then he spoke.

"Well, I can certainly vibe with that . . . especially if it includes Howard," he said.

I swear my brain started singing. It was as if Victoria was looking over this table and willing the truth to finally create some good between my father and me. I went back to chewing my food, which was hard to do while I was smiling so broadly. In between bites, Dad and I exchanged laughs and jokes. It was the best family dinner I remembered having in some time. We started getting ready to leave, and the server came by to bring the check. I finally caught a look at her face.

"How was everything?" she asked. Sheila, better known as Victoria, winked.

"Just great," I responded.

CHAPTER SEVENTEEN

✦✦
✦

I came home from dinner feeling more at peace than I'd felt in months. I had nothing to worry about—except for the usual schoolwork, what my next newspaper story could be after my big *Featherstone Post* exclusive, and what hair cream worked best to keep my edges flat during gym class. No friend drama, no field hockey, no *How am I going to make Dad happy if I don't go to Howard?*

I went to my room, put on my pajamas, and got ready for bed. I figured I'd do some reading or text with Chloe before I fell asleep. I fished out my journal, which was safely locked in my nightstand, and recapped everything that had happened over the past few weeks.

Dear Journal,

Seems like things are looking up. Apology tour is done, and I broke the biggest story the <u>Featherstone Post</u> has ever published. And my family hasn't gotten any hate mail or been run out of town over it. In fact, another school asked me to speak to their sixth-grade history classes about my family history! Nia and I are back on track. I told my dad about racist Ginny and the Chadwick Boseman drama school at

Howard. I never did get to tell Lee how I'd felt about him. But I did apologize. And I babysat Chadwick last week while Lee was at Creeks club, and it wasn't so bad. I fed Chadwick some twigs and berries. I scratched his back. Mostly he sleeps a lot. I got my homework done. Everyone wins. And he's not even that scaly.

Speaking of, when is Victoria going to lift that spell already? I've done every darn thing she's asked. And then some!

Just then I felt a breeze in my room. The papers and notebooks I had stacked on the corner of my desk blew around. A fog crawled in front of me, the same hazy, dusty glow that probably popped up after magical unicorns trampled through a field of wildflowers. It began to fall from the ceiling and then swirl around into a funnel cone. Then it took the shape of a woman. Ah, the usual visit from my fairy godmother. Victoria.

For the first time since she'd put that spell on me, I didn't feel a pang of anxiety or the weight of dread that I usually felt when she dropped in on me. I had done everything she'd asked. I was truthful with everyone about my feelings about the apology and about school. About my family. She had no reason to scold me.

"What's up, Victoria?" I said smugly. I usually didn't

greet her first. "Are you here to call me out on some truths? I have truth receipts for you for days!"

"I know," she said. "And I am very, very proud of you. The newspaper article was amazing. The conversation with your dad at the Crab Shack, even better."

"But I know you saw that firsthand, *Sheila*."

She smirked. "Right, that's right."

"Why do you keep spying on me there?" I asked. "As a waitress! There's gotta be an easier way."

Victoria looked at me. She sat down on the edge of my bed. "Okay, I'll tell you the truth for a change. The truth is that I like waitressing. It's a good job. It tips well."

I twisted my lips. "You need money where you're from in Fairy Godmotherland? Don't you all just wave your magic wands and get whatever you want up there?"

"Okay, fine, we do," she said. "I just like meeting new people, okay?"

"But they can't see you when you're in fairy god-mother form."

"Well, that's neither here nor there," she said. "*Anyway!* I have witnessed what you've been doing over the last couple of days, and I must say you've made great progress. As I promised, if you personally apologized to everyone at camp, I would lift the spell. And so the time has come."

I looked at her with wide eyes. "Does this mean—does this mean what I think it means?"

"Yes, June. It means you're free from the spell."

I shot up from my desk chair. I couldn't believe it. Freedom of speech! The freedom to tell the truth, the little truths, the big truths, and everything in between. I felt a rush of hope, of anticipation for a future without boundaries, without someone keeping watch over me at all times (including in the bathroom!). I was stoked to get some privacy back. I was also super excited to be able to react and respond to things without the wrath of the truth police.

Speaking of truth, did living without the spell mean I could lie again? I hadn't come this far just so I could lie again, right? I mean, that's why Victoria had come into my life in the first place, to teach me that lying is not the way to live happily. And when I hid my feelings, that had gotten me in trouble (*see:* leaked blog, Lee and Nia drama). But at least I could edit my feelings, right? Or could I create, like, different versions of myself, like Beyoncé does with Sasha Fierce? So that I could have the freedom to say things that maybe June wouldn't be comfortable sharing but *Janae* might be! That could give me the freedom to make up stories again, to create fantastical worlds, write fiction, tell . . . well, not lies, but embellishments! Like, harmless little white lies! But again, that felt . . . awkward? Like perhaps I misunderstood the entire point of the spell in the first place?

I sat with myself for a second and closed my eyes. I took a breath and thought about what I was truly feeling now that I knew the spell was gone. I actually felt the same as I did five minutes earlier, before I knew I was out from under the spell. But still, the freedom was thrilling.

"Wow, it feels so . . . normal?"

Victoria laughed. "Well, maybe that's because the spell has been lifted for some time now."

I tilted my head and scrunched my eyebrows. "What do you mean?"

"I lifted the spell right after you came home from camp, as promised. I watched you approach people one by one and apologize. And you held steady even when they didn't respond nicely. But even then, I noticed that you kept telling the truth without being under the spell. You wrote the story about your family, even though you knew it could be emotionally difficult for the entire town. You told the truth to your friends. You told the truth to your mom about being nervous about writing the story, and you even told the truth to your dad about your feelings about Howard, your feelings about the creative arts. And through it all, you've been . . . relaxed. You really have learned your lesson."

"So you're saying that the curse has been gone for weeks already?!" I asked. "Am I really free?"

"Yep," she said, and beamed.

I looked at her, confused. "If the curse is gone, why are you still here?"

Victoria got up from her seat on the edge of my bed and walked across my room. "I debated telling you sooner, but you had that issue of the school paper, and then your father took you out to dinner. I wanted to make sure you'd really learned your lesson. But after seeing you with your dad tonight, I'm convinced. Spell was dropped. Spell will stay dropped."

I rolled my shoulders back. I felt like I'd just been sprung from detention or time-out. "So, what happens now?" I asked. "Are you still going to visit me every so often? Or watch my every move?"

Victoria walked back to me. "My presence in your life will depend on your behavior. If you continue living your truth and being honest and open with people in a respectful manner, my visits to your bedroom or your school will be few and far between. However, if you start to slip into your old ways, I may pay you a not-so-private visit in a not-so-private place to remind you of all the good work you've accomplished so far."

I'd almost forgotten what life was like without having these random fairy-dust storms of Victoria's every so often. It really was like having a guardian angel on my shoulder, even if she did kick up quite a mess sometimes.

I nodded slowly. I remembered how scared I was when we'd first met each other in that fun house during the fall carnival. How I'd cried to Nia and Chloe about my inability to tell little white lies. I didn't think I'd survive it. I thought I'd embarrass myself ten times over. (And I did. But I lived.) Before, I was too scared to tell the truth for fear of hurting people's feelings. But when I tried to hide the truth, I managed to hurt every single person in town with my secret blog. Somehow I fixed things, we all healed, and I came out okay. No matter what, I came out okay.

"I never thought I would say this, but thank you," I said. "I probably would have continued telling people lies for a long time, maybe the rest of my life, if you hadn't come and showed me another way."

"And that was the goal," Victoria said. "We all have things about ourselves that we don't like, that we may feel some guilt or shame about. But that doesn't mean we should hide those things from ourselves or others. And just because you disagree with other people on certain things doesn't mean that you should hide your feelings from them."

"Victoria . . . is this goodbye?" I said.

"No, it's not goodbye," she said, putting a hand on my shoulder. "It's 'see you later.'"

And with that, she backed away, turning herself into fairy dust one more time and disappearing into thin air before my eyes.

CHAPTER EIGHTEEN

✦ ✦
✦

Wednesday morning, I did something I hadn't done in months. I picked up the phone and sent a text to Nia.

> **JUNE:** Hey. Walking to school? Should I wait for you?

I finally had the nerve and the confidence to have a deep chat with her since the blog leak. We were back on speaking terms, but since Victoria had removed the spell, I wanted Nia to know what I truly thought about our friendship. Also I knew Olive had to go to school early for some orchestra thing, so there was a good chance Nia would be walking alone.

> **NIA:** Meet you at the end of your driveway

I went to my closet, looking for something bold and sunny to match my mood—my yellow tennis dress and white Nikes. We were past spring break, and it was finally warm and beautiful outside. I went back to my room and grabbed my things for school, then went downstairs for breakfast.

Our housekeeper, Luisa, had made scrambled eggs and sliced a bunch of fruit for us, so I got myself a plate. I ate quickly, not wanting to keep Nia waiting, and thought about what I was going to say so it came out smoothly.

Mom sat next to me at the kitchen table and joined me for a quick breakfast.

"Nia's walking to school with me today," I told her.

"So things are back to normal with you two?"

"Some things," I said, finishing my eggs in record time and then grabbing my bag to head out.

I walked outside and waited at the end of my driveway. Nia was walking up toward me.

"How are you?" she asked.

"Things are good. Guess what? Victoria lifted the spell!"

"Get out!" Nia said. "How? Why?"

"She told me I had learned how to tell the truth. She watched me do it. She'd said she would lift the spell if I personally apologized to everyone I talked about in the blog, and I did. I feel like I earned my life back."

"Nice," she said. "Kinda stressful to have somebody watching over you all the time, right?"

"Tell me about it. She'll still pop in sometimes, she said. Who knows?"

A few minutes passed. Nia stayed mostly quiet during the walk, looking at trees and kids as they passed by.

I decided to finally ask the other burning question I was dying to know the answer to.

"So, what's going on with you and Lee?"

I braced myself for her to say they were officially a couple and that they had Sunday dinner together every week. *It's okay. The truth can't hurt me anymore. Just fire away.*

"Nothing's going on," Nia said. "He's around, I'm around."

I was confused. "You guys haven't, like, hung out?"

"I mean, we talk at school. Maybe I've seen him after school once, but, like, it hasn't been some big dating thing. Besides, I know that you got feelings for him."

Say what? All the drama, all the time not speaking, and it turned out they weren't even hanging out?

"Well, I mean, I *did* think—kinda sorta, ahem . . . but I don't know exactly how I feel. That is the truth."

Nia turned to me. "Well, anyway, I know how *I* feel, and I feel like I'm chill on Lee."

Wow, okay, wow. This was not the conversation I thought we'd have. Nia was basically admitting she decided not to pursue anything with Lee because she knew I liked him. This was huge. This whole time I'd assumed she was stealing him away from me—but she knew how I felt all along, and she chose to honor our friendship over a boy.

"I mean, Lee wasn't like my boyfriend or anything," I said.

"I know, girl, but just . . . it's just better this way."

I was playing it cool on the outside, but my heart was doing jumping jacks. It was like all my internal organs were hugging each other. Did this mean that I could still hold on to that fantasy I had of Lee and me living in Featherstone Creek as mayor and first lady? I wondered if I would start having those dreams about us getting married again.

But then I remembered Alvin, and how close we'd gotten during the musical, and how nice and funny and talented he was, and the fact that I'd invited him over to my house anytime. Ugh, was I going to choose between them now?! *Take a breath, June. . . .*

"Changing the subject," I said, because I honestly wanted to change the subject, "what's going on with basketball and stuff?"

"We're pretty much done. Games ended right before the trip."

"Oh, gotcha," I said sheepishly. "Does that mean we get to hang out more?"

"Yeah," Nia said. "I was going to hang out with Erica and Keisha after school today. They asked me to go shopping or something. Erica does all this fashion stuff on TikTok."

"Erica and Keisha," I said. They were in the sixth grade, too. I'd met them at school a few times, and they'd always seemed friendly. "Are they your new friends?"

"Well, they like clothes. We talk about music and stuff. . . . They're cool, you know."

"That's cool if you want to hang out with them," I said, feeling a little slighted but still happy that Nia had friends with similar interests.

Nia gave me a sympathetic look. "Listen, I mean, I

think it's okay if we, like, have other friends. Like, you and Alvin do stuff together. I could do stuff with other people. And it doesn't mean I don't want to hang with you."

I struggled to put the right words together. My heart felt heavy as I thought about spending less time with someone I'd spent every birthday, weekend, and Disney movie release with since, basically, I was born. Was this the end of Nia and me? Couldn't be. Maybe it was just a change. "Yeah. No. I'm not saying that we *have* to do everything together, but, like . . . friendships change and evolve. Well, that's what I heard on this podcast the other day, anyway."

I looked around for Victoria. This seemed like one of those times when a sprinkle of fairy dust might magically fly up my nose to remind me to be truthful but kind. I loved Nia—she was probably the closest friend I had in Featherstone Creek. But I had a feeling that we were growing in different directions. Not apart—headed the same way, but on different roads.

I turned to her. "I want us to stay friends. I've known you my whole life. You're like a sister to me. But sometimes sisters aren't best friends, though they love each other unconditionally and have each other's backs. Maybe we're more like sisters?"

"Yeah, June. I see that," Nia said. "You are my sister, and I love you a lot."

"Yeah," I said. "And sometimes we say not-so-nice things to each other, but it's okay because it's all out of love and because we care. And I know I've said some things and I'm sorry."

Nia looked at me. "I'm sorry, too. I don't know why I act out some-

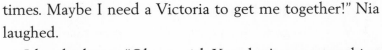

times. Maybe I need a Victoria to get me together!" Nia laughed.

I laughed, too. "Oh no, girl. You don't want anything that extreme showing up in your life. Besides, I've always got your back."

"Yeah," Nia said. "I've always got your back, too."

We arrived at school and set out on our separate ways for our lockers.

"Meet you in homeroom?" Nia asked.

"See you there," I said.

CHAPTER NINETEEN

✦ ✦
✦

Warmer weather had finally arrived post–spring break, my big story in the *Post* had been well received, and my overall fortunes had reversed. I felt like celebrating. I convinced my parents to have a group dinner at our house with my friends and their parents, just like old times. We planned a barbecue for Saturday evening.

I wanted to invite my friends when I saw them at school, but it turned out that my parents were quicker at sending invites than I was. My dad had already told Nia's and Blake's dads about the dinner plan at work, since they all worked at the same firm. I invited Olive in homeroom, and she accepted. It was an official reunion.

Well, almost. I thought about whether to invite Lee

and Alvin, the two people who I had the most conflicted feelings about. Would it be weird to have them at my house after everything that had happened? After everything I had said to both of them? I mean, we saw each other at school, sure, but my home was different. It was my personal space.

Neither of those things mattered—when I came home Friday night, my mom had already invited Lee and his grandparents. And if Lee was coming, then Alvin needed to come, too—one, it would make it less weird for me, and, two, it would make it less weird for Lee, so he wasn't the only boy in the group.

And I knew Lee was definitely coming because Mom had promised to make her famous 7UP cake, which he loved. (I did not. I'd already admitted this to my mom in the early days of the truth-telling spell!)

When Saturday arrived, I was so excited that it felt like Christmas morning. We hadn't all been to-gether for dinner since the holidays. I sprang out of bed, eager to get everything in the house ready for my friends.

As I looked at my-self in the mirror while

brushing my teeth, I realized it had been a few days since I'd seen Victoria. I hadn't heard from her, or seen her in the form of anyone or anything else, since she'd said goodbye. There hadn't even been a twinkle of fairy dust. I couldn't believe I was admitting this, but I sort of missed her. *Sort* of.

On Saturday afternoon, I helped Mom with some housework and cleaned up around the backyard. It was sandals-without-socks warm. I had on a short-sleeve shirt and jeans, and the sun was pleasantly warm on my skin.

Nia was the first one to arrive at the house. Her dad had volunteered to bring his baby back ribs, and he was carrying a platter of charred meat smothered in barbecue sauce. Nia's mom brought a salad and gave one-armed hugs and kisses on the cheek as she walked to the kitchen. "I'm glad to see you and Nia back on good terms," she said to me with a smile.

What do you say to the mother of the girl who leaked your personal diary to the world, leaving you exposed and embarrassed? "Yes, ma'am" was all I could come up with. Nia and I had called a truce, after all. I could only keep the peace. I might never forget what she'd done, but I'd forgiven her—it was time to move on.

Nia, in black jeans and a glittery top, walked in behind her mom. "You look nice," she told me. I complimented her shimmery pink nails, which looked like she'd just painted them before she came over. We kept it polite and casual and light between us. We were both tired of the drama and happy for the good food ahead.

Olive and her parents arrived after Nia. Olive beelined straight for us in the backyard. "Hiiii," she said. "I brought snacks. We good today?"

"Yes, Olive," I said. Nia and I both gave silly grins at the same time.

We took turns on the trampoline while we waited for the rest of our guests to arrive, then checked out Instagram on Nia's phone. (I was still off social media since

the blog leak.) After that, we went looking around the garage for my old Hula-Hoops and roller skates. We saw Lee and Alvin arrive when we were in the garage playing, and the boys joined us while Lee's grandparents and Alvin's mother went inside.

The distraction of random items in our garage meant I didn't have to immediately face Lee or Alvin and wonder what they were going to say. Or not say. The boys threw a football back and forth while Nia and Olive watched. I excused myself to go inside to grab my phone.

I cut through the kitchen and I saw my mom and Nia's mom standing there, talking in hushed tones. "It was time the full story was told," my mom said. I assumed they were talking about the Featherstone Creek founders story.

"And your June was sure the right one to do it. She's such a bright girl," Nia's mom said. I blushed. I was honored she thought of me that way. She clearly hadn't seen my secret blog. Because if I were Nia's mom and had read what was written about my child on that blog, I wouldn't have been so nice about it. I'd said so many mean things about Nia. I also might have said something about Nia's mom, too? Something about her senior citizen shoes? Ugh, that blog would haunt me for life. . . . I clenched my eyes shut.

"I don't know what's going on with Nia lately," Nia's mom said, changing the subject. I unclenched my eyes.

"It's just this life stage," Mom said. "It's hard. Give her some time. She'll come around."

"No, it's more than that. I had to send her to a counselor a few weeks ago. She's been more than a handful."

A "handful"? Was that parent code for troublemaker? Disobedient? I mean, yes, Nia could be kinda tough. Her getting me canceled by revealing my secret blog hadn't felt so good. And I had seen Nia leaving the school therapist's office a few weeks ago. Did that have anything to do with what Nia's mom was talking about?

I wondered if that was the reason Nia had been so snippy to me. Was that why she'd leaked the blog? Taken out such massive revenge on me rather than just yelling at me in private and not speaking to me in public, like most sixth graders would have done if they'd gotten into a fight with their best friend? I wondered what was up. I wondered if I could help her in some way.

"Well, she is eleven. Maybe she's just starting to go through puberty," my mom said.

Puberty?!

"Could be," Nia's mom said. "It is about that time, huh? Soon I'll have to buy her a bra."

Whoa. I mean, Nia was always the one who seemed to know everything before Olive and I did. Could she be the first to get everything else, too? To get her period? To shave her legs? Maybe she'd already done some of those things. Maybe that was why she was cranky. Maybe we really were going our separate ways as she matured and left the rest of us behind.

I slunk away from the kitchen and shook my head, trying to unhear what I'd heard the moms talking about. Even though Nia and I had acknowledged we might be giving each other some space, I didn't want to think about her growing apart from me just yet.

Blake and her family arrived just as dinner was being served. The gang and I sat around a large picnic table while the parents gathered at several other patio tables, enjoying plates of ribs, chicken, salad, and fruits. It felt magical, all my friends gathered around, eating, laughing, and enjoying the springtime weather.

Nia politely pushed her plate away and leaned back and spoke over the giggling. "A'ight, so, like . . . now what?"

The rest of us looked confused. "Dessert?" I asked.

"No, silly," she said. "I mean, what do we have to look forward to now? The musical is over. The spring trip's over. We need something else to do. I feel like we need to make something. Something, I don't know . . . creative?"

"Oh, like an underground blog that holds all our secrets?" I joked. Maybe I felt overconfident because I was

in my own house and everyone's parents were within earshot. I smiled wide, like a clown, overemphasizing that I was just joking.

"Oh no no. We see what happens with those!" Olive laughed.

"Maybe we could create a secret private social network instead?" Alvin offered.

"I'm done with secrets," I said. "I've kept enough of those."

Lee put down his fork. "What about a book club?" he suggested. "But, like, a cool one. With, like, spy books and how-to guides and stuff."

"I like it," Blake said. "And ours can be cooler than, like, reading a chapter and then discussing it over chai lattes and cake," she added.

"What's wrong with cake?" Lee asked in between chomping large bites of rib meat.

"Don't we already have enough reading for our English lit class?" Nia asked.

"No, we'll choose books they'd never pick for class. Like comics. Good books," I said. "Things we actually want to read."

"To be honest, I've always wanted to read Kwame Alexander's books but haven't gotten around to doing it yet," Blake said. "This will be fun."

"So we're creating a book club to give ourselves more

homework than we already have?" Nia said. "I am not seeing the point."

"It's also a good reason to hang out together and talk about things we don't want our parents to know," Olive said. "Besides, if we ask our parents to take us to book club, they'll never say no or 'maybe later.' They'll always be down to help us read more!"

"True," Nia said. "So where should we meet?"

"Here," I offered. "Or we can go to different places. Or . . . we could meet at the ice cream place, and then we'd get money for ice cream every time. So we can get ice cream *and* hang out."

"Smart—I like that," Alvin said.

"All right, so we need a name."

We started throwing out names. "Bookmania!" Olive shouted.

"Best Book Club!" Blake added.

"How about Not Your Parents' Book Club?" I said, stealing a glance at our parents across the yard.

"Oh, that's good!" Nia said.

Everyone agreed. Decision made. "Should we make T-shirts?" Blake asked.

"Let's pick the first book," Lee said.

We spent the rest of the night debating which books to pick, in between doing random TikTok dance challenges and jumping on my trampoline, daring each other to take bigger jumps and do higher flips until Nia claimed she sprained her ankle doing a back handspring. In the end we decided on *Black Boy Joy*, mostly because we liked the title. We all committed to the book, and I grabbed some ice for Nia's ankle, and we sat and laughed and watched our parents laugh too loud at whatever they thought was funny (which was usually not the same thing that we found funny) until the evening wound down. When the last guest left—Nia, hobbling out with her parents—I realized I'd had my first drama-, headache- and stomachache-free time with good friends in quite a while. No weirdness, no lies, no hard feelings, and no fairy dust causing me to sneeze like a hyena. And it felt really, really good.

CHAPTER TWENTY

+ +
+

I retreated to my bedroom after dinner. I was ready to pass out from eating what seemed like an entire platter of ribs, corn, and even a small slice of Mom's cake. (It was actually pretty good this time.) Despite feeling bloated, I was content. Tomorrow was Sunday, so there was no school. I had resolved all of the big issues with my closest friends. The only thing on my mind—and I couldn't believe I was thinking this—was that I kinda sorta maybe missed Victoria.

I wondered when I would see her again. I couldn't even believe we'd met each other in the first place. How had she found me? Why me? She must have been watching me for months before she decided I was the one she needed to throw this spell on. Which meant she was probably following me now. She was totally watching to make sure I was still telling the truth. She did say she'd still be "around."

I scanned my room. I looked in the corners, around my desk, in my closet, my dresser, for any signs of Victoria. I looked at my pictures. Had she shape-shifted into the image of my cousin in the framed photo on my dresser, or Beyoncé in the poster on my wall? Nope, everything seemed pretty normal.

Suddenly my phone beeped from the corner of my desk, where I was charging it.

The home screen lit up with a text from Blake.

> **BLAKE:** Things seemed good with Nia tonight! And good job naming the book club!

> **JUNE:** Thx girl.

I took a deep breath in and caught a glimpse of myself in the mirror. I smiled back at the person I saw. I felt . . . comfortable. Except for the small twig in my hair and the flyaways around my head from jumping on my trampoline with my friends. I needed a shower.

I headed to the bath-
room to clean up, wash
my face, and change into
my pajamas. Saturday
night usually meant stay-
ing up well past bed-
time to watch movies
or YouTube or to read,
but tonight I was tired
pretty early. A good kind of

tired, the tired you feel after running
around at the beach or doing something just as fun.

I walked over to the picture of Lee and me on my
desk and reached to the back, loosening the key from the
frame. Then I pulled my journal out from under the mattress and crawled into bed.

I wrote a few lines in my journal, the secret stash for
all my musings since the blog had been leaked.

Dear Journal,

Is everything really all good? It almost seems too
good to be true. Maybe it's just a moment of peace
for everyone right now. For now I should be grateful.
Grateful that I can tell the truth to everyone and not
feel anxiety over it. Grateful that I realized I didn't have

to keep saying things just to make people happy or to keep friends. The truth—told directly, kindly, to people's faces—is better.

Except about boys. True feelings about boys should stay in journals. Or else you end up saying "right back atcha" to boys you may or may not like and look like a fool and then they're too embarrassed to sit next to you on the bus ride back from the camping trip. That is, until you invite them to jump on your trampoline. No boy can resist jumping on a trampoline.

I closed the journal, locked it up, and put it back under my mattress. I got up and returned the key to its secret hiding place. And then I wondered, *What happens now?*

Over the past few months, I'd come face to face with things that I didn't like about myself, as well as things that I didn't know I *did* like about myself. I'd discovered things I wanted to tell people, or should have never told people but did. Some of those things really, truly hurt others. Some of those things hurt me most of all. But here I was. I didn't have headaches and stomachaches as often as I used to. I breathed much easier during school. My friendships were stronger. My grades were better. And my parents even seemed happier with me. Maybe telling the truth wasn't all that bad.

But maybe telling a white lie here and there wouldn't be all that bad, either. I mean, can one tell the truth all the time, forever and ever? Was Victoria really still watching me, or was she back in Fairy Godmotherville?

I was sure she was bluffing. She'd probably moved on from me and found someone else to put her spell on. She would probably forget all about me. She'd probably never return, never sprinkle fairy dust in my cornflakes to remind me to tell the truth. She had probably already found another eleven-year-old to teach this lesson to. My fairy godmother had left me to watch over some other

half-truth-telling kid! Never to return and leaving me free to be, and say, whatever I wanted.

I started to think of my future without Victoria. To think we wouldn't see each other again. To think I'd actually eat nachos at the Crab Shack and not have an allergy attack.

I leaned back on my bed. My stomach started to rumble. My nose itched.

I smiled.

I knew you wouldn't forget me, Victoria.

Acknowledgments

I will forever be grateful to Kate Udvari and Ann Maranzano for their support and partnership. To Sasha Henriques and Michelle Nagler, thank you for helping me bring June Jackson to life! It has been such a pleasure to work with you, and I can't wait to see where June's adventures take her.

Stef, I am so lucky to collaborate with you. Thank you for all the late-night sessions and marathon calls. I couldn't ask for a better writing partner.

Brittney, thank you for your beautiful illustrations. I know my readers will fall in love with them, too.

To André Des Rochers, Bejidé Davis, and the entire Granderson Des Rochers family, thank you for your continued support and counsel throughout this process.

To Phoebe, thank you for all the texting and FaceTiming

to help me get June just right. It's my honor and privilege to write for you and girls just like you.

To my family: Mom, Dad, Adrianne, Erica, Lisa, and William, I am lucky to be a member of the best tribe. Thank you for all your love and support.

To Cristiano, eu te amo sempre. As we always say, "sempre juntos."

To Michelle, I thank you always because I just wouldn't survive without you! You are the best cousin/friend a girl could ask for, and I had Blake in mind the entire time I was working on this project.

To all my dear friends, I am so lucky to do life with you. Thank you for the laughter and love that fuel my creativity.

Finally, to my readers, there will never be enough thank-yous for your emails, posts, and support. Here's to more writing adventures.

ABOUT THE AUTHOR AND ILLUSTRATOR

Tina Wells is the founder of RLVNT Media, a multimedia content venture serving entrepreneurs, tweens, and culturists with authentic representation. Tina has been named one of *Fast Company*'s 100 Most Creative People in Business, has been listed in *Essence*'s 40 Under 40, and has received *Cosmopolitan*'s Fun Fearless Phenom Award, among many honors. She is the author of nine books, including the bestselling tween fiction series Mackenzie Blue; its spinoff series, The Zee Files; and the marketing handbook *Chasing Youth Culture and Getting It Right*.

Brittney Bond was born in sunny South Florida to a Jamaican family. A self-taught artist, she works primarily digitally, with a passion for using appealing color palettes, intriguing lighting, and a magical and positive aura throughout her illustrations.

Check out more Honest June!
Honestly, you don't want to miss it.

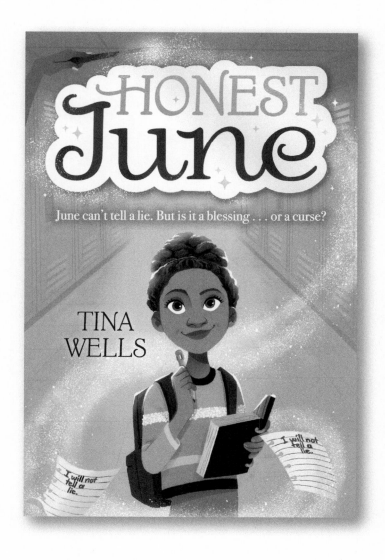

CHAPTER ONE

✦ ✦
✦

I don't know everything about life yet, but I know at least one thing is true—life's easier when you make people happy.

You want to get good grades? Tell teachers what they want to hear. Want your friends to like you? Tell them you love their clothes and their hair and their moms' cooking. Want your parents to be happy? Do what they say. Follow their rules. Happy parents equals extra dessert and cool toys and fun vacations. And, most importantly, love.

Making people happy is what I'm good at. Sometimes that means not telling people the whole truth. Or telling them no truth at all. Not because I'm trying to be mischievous! In fact, I don't like to make trouble—but it always finds me somehow. Like the time I tried to compliment my best friend Nia on a pair of shoes she was wearing. I said they made her feet look "too long." She was mad at me for a week. I vowed to say only nice things about her feet no matter what.

Or the time I accidentally knocked over the mailbox when Dad asked me to take out the trash. Instead of walking it to the corner, I put the trash bag on my old wagon to roll it down the driveway. I had the wagon aimed perfectly at the mailbox to stop its roll, but it smacked into the pole harder than I expected, knocking the mailbox over at a forty-five-degree angle. Oops! I went inside and pretended nothing happened. But the next morning, Dad was furious. His eyebrows came together in the middle of his forehead. "Stupid garbage trucks! I'm going to find out who did this and get them fired," he said. I stood there, silent. What if he found out it was me? Would he fire me as his daughter? I kept my mouth shut. He fixed the mailbox and forgot about it in a few days, thankfully.

Or the time my mother asked me if I knew what the "birds and the bees" was, and I told her the truth—"No. Should I?" This led to one of the most uncomfortable conversations of my life about boys and girls and babies and . . . *ugh!* I get the heebie-jeebies every time I think about it!

I've found in my brief eleven years on this earth that the truth isn't always necessary. Tell people what they want to hear. Smile and nod. No one gets hurt. And that is how I planned to get through the sixth grade, through middle school, and through the rest of my life.

✦

It was the Sunday of Labor Day weekend, two days before the end of summer vacation. But in Featherstone Creek, a suburb of Atlanta, the weather stays warm through fall—so it still feels just a bit like summer outside. Mom, Dad, and I got back home from our house at Lake Lanier, about an hour's drive away, late at night—just in time for me to unload my bags, eat a spoonful of peanut butter, put on my pajamas, and immediately pass out. I don't even remember if I brushed my teeth. I slept like I hadn't slept for ten years, and I didn't wake up until I heard the chime notification from Nia's text on my phone.

> **NIA:** You there? We're coming at 5 p.m. today.

I jumped out of bed and got dressed. My best friends Nia Shorter and Olive Banks were coming over for one last summer barbecue before school started. We were going to celebrate as if it were our birthdays and New Year's

Eve combined. After tonight, we had only one more day of no homework, no teachers, no alarms to wake up to before . . . *it begins.*

"It" being our first day of the sixth grade and our first day at Featherstone Creek Middle School.

We were no longer grade-schoolers. This was middle school. Prime time. The big leagues. At FCMS, we needed to bring our A games. We needed to make a great—scratch that, *legendary*—impression from day one and live up to the legacies that our parents and grandparents had created for us. Or else our parents would be disappointed. Our neighbors wouldn't like us. Teachers wouldn't like us. Then colleges wouldn't like us. And we wouldn't get degrees. And then we wouldn't be able to get good jobs, and we'd have no money or friends or husbands, and we'd be living on our parents' couches forever, surviving on chicken wings and Flamin' Hot Cheetos. And then we'd become embarrassments to our families. If, at that point, our families still claimed us.

Okay, maybe not all these things would happen if we didn't rock middle school. I tend to overthink things sometimes . . . just part of my charm, I guess? I don't really like Cheetos anyway!

I straightened up my bedroom, which was next to Dad's office. I kept my room nice and neat so my parents wouldn't be tempted to come in and rifle through my things, like my journals or my laptop or—*gasp*—my phone.

If they thought I kept my room in order, they'd think I kept my life in order, too. I smoothed my sheets and comforter and arranged all the pillows from large to small against the headboard. I cleaned my desk and straightened my framed photos of me and Nia and me and my BFF Chloe Lawrence-Johnson, who I've known since I was a baby but who moved to Los Angeles with her family last year. I went into my bathroom and put away the bottles of leave-in conditioner and edge gel I used on my hair today to put it up into a high braided bun—my go-to hairstyle for a summertime barbecue. Tomorrow, the day before school, is wash day.

By the time I made it downstairs, my stomach was already rumbling, and my mom and dad were almost set getting food ready for the barbecue. My dad, wearing an old Howard University T-shirt and jeans, stood at the kitchen counter over a huge platter of chicken covered with barbecue sauce. My dad is a lawyer. He went to school with Nia's dad at THE Howard University, aka the Harvard of the HBCUs, aka the Mecca, according to Dad. He practically screams "H-U! You *knowwwwww!*" if anyone merely thinks about Howard in the same room as him. And he has big plans for his little girl to follow in his footsteps. Every. Single. One. He runs a law firm together with Nia's dad in downtown Featherstone Creek, with their last names on the front of their office building.

Dad wants me to either run his firm when he retires or head into politics, like Madam Vice President Kamala Harris ("H-U '86!" my dad screams at any mention of her name). I like wearing and buying nice clothes, and I definitely love MVP Harris, but I don't know how I feel about arguing with people all the time, which is what legal stuff seems to be about, at least to me. And those suits they wear in court. They're so stiff and itchy! And lady lawyers have to wear pantyhose even on hot summer days in Atlanta. Meanwhile, I get uncomfortable in jean shorts in July sometimes!

My mom is a doctor who delivers babies for all the moms in town. She works a lot, but she gets to hold babies all the time, which sounds awesome. Her family grew up in Featherstone Creek, and most of them started businesses here. Her dad, my granddad, has a family practice on Main Street. He's our family doctor and Nia's family doctor. And the doctor for half of my sixth-grade class.

My parents always mean well—they want the best for me—and I want to make them happy. Because when they're happy, the house is happy. We eat ice cream and go to the Crab Shack for dinner. And spend more time at our lake house, and my mom and I get our nails done together at the salon. And my dad laughs with his mouth wide open, and when he laughs, everyone else laughs. When my parents aren't happy, there are rain clouds, and boiled brussels sprouts for dinner, and my mom calls me by my full name—"June Naomi Jackson!"—in a high-pitched voice, and my dad's eyebrows come together on his forehead like one long, hairy caterpillar. The eyebrows scare. The. Life. Out. Of. Me.

So, if me playing field hockey, going to Howard, and being a lawyer are what's going to make them happy, then that's what I'll do. Or at least I'll *say* it's what I want to do. But a girl has a right to her own opinions. And a right to change her own opinions, too. Even if she keeps them to herself, which I am very used to doing.

At 5:00 p.m. the doorbell rang. Mr. and Mrs. Shorter and Nia stood at the door. Mrs. Shorter held a large Tupperware bowl of potato salad for dinner. "Hello, June, how are you, baby? Oh, you're getting so tall," she said.

"Hi, Mrs. Shorter. My mom is in the kitchen."

"Smells good back there," Mr. Shorter said, giving me a gentle hug. Nia's parents walked toward the back of the house. Nia put an arm around me. "Girl! I thought you'd never come back!"

"We texted every day I was gone!" I said. She and Olive and I texted multiple times a day, all through summer. We basically knew where each other was at every second of the day. Nia rolled her eyes and smiled. We both giggled and ran upstairs to my bedroom. I flopped onto the bed, and Nia followed me, placing her bag down next to her.

"Sixth grade," I said. "Finally, a place where I can really express myself." I could use different-colored gel pens for my homework. Explore creative writing, join the school paper, really voice my opinions on big issues, like going vegan and saving the animals. Maybe I'd run for student body president. And I could even buy my own lunch! Freedom—I'd *literally* be able to taste it. "I'll be glad to get out from under my parents' wing," I said.

"You act as if you're going off to college," Nia said.

"They still feed you and give you an allowance." Ugh. She was *technically* right. But at least I could choose one of my own daily meals at school! That would be a taste of freedom—it had to count for something.

"Did you read the books on the summer reading list?" I asked.

"I only made it through one," Nia answered.

"Which one?"

"The shortest one. Something about the guy with the dog. It said the reading was optional."

"Optional, but encouraged," I said resolutely. I chose to read half the books on the list, though they, too, were the shortest ones. Even if teachers weren't assigning the book list as a requirement, it could only make them happy to know you did some of the reading. It might help me get in good with these teachers from the beginning. I could use all the early bonus points I could get.

A knock on the door interrupted our conversation. "It's me," Olive called out. "Sorry we're late. Mom couldn't decide what to wear. What's going on?" she asked as she opened the door, walked in, and plopped onto my bed.

"We're talking about school," I said.

"Yeah? I'm excited. Orchestra starts up again next week. I learned how to play Michael Jackson's 'Beat It' on the viola this summer."

"On to the most important topic," Nia interrupted. "What are you going to wear for the first day?"

I stood up and threw open the doors to my closet. Mom and I had gone shopping for new clothes the week before we went to Lake Lanier. She took me to the same stores where she's bought clothes for me since I was four.

"This would look so cute on you," Mom had said, holding up a pleated skirt with a printed pattern of teddy bears with their paws in honey jars. It looked like what preschoolers in the Alps might wear as part of their school wardrobe. I hated it.

I clenched my teeth. "It's cute, Mom, very cute." She tossed it into the shopping cart. I groaned internally, but I figured if I let her pick out one thing she liked, maybe I could get what I really wanted.

I wanted to go to stores that aligned more with my sense of style. This place called Fit sold women's clothes and accessories and just about every item I'd seen on some influencer or celebrity on Instagram. I pointed to a dress on a mannequin in the store window as we passed by. "I saw this dress on that dark-haired Disney Channel actress you like, and she's my age."

"Yeah, but she's an actress, playing a role. You are in sixth grade, and I don't know if I want you wearing that. It's a bit . . . mature."

"That's the point," I said. "*I'm* a bit mature now." I'm in sixth freaking grade! I am almost in a training bra! Can't she see I'm practically a *woman*?

I walked inside. There was a white sleeveless blouse

with a large bow at the neck that could pair with everything in my closet and still make me look sophisticated, even with that horrible teddy bear skirt my mom bought. But I really wanted to wear it with the pair of distressed jeans on display that had a few holes around the knees that . . . oh, look at that . . . came in my size.

She ended up buying me the blouse on the condition that I wear a sweater or jacket over it. She got her baby skirt, and I got my blouse. Everybody was happy. *Compromise.*

"So, the first day of school," Nia said. She and Olive looked at my clothes hanging neatly in my closet. "Are we doing the skinny jeans with the oversized T-shirt thing? Maybe with those Air Force 1s? Or with a shiny ballet flat? You need something that will really make a statement on the first day."

"I want something that says I'm . . . interesting," I said thoughtfully.

"Soooo, black on black on black?" Nia smirked.

"Or maybe a caftan?" Olive said.

"A caftan?" Nia asked.

"Yeah, like what my grandmother wears exclusively from April through October. She says they let her skin breathe," Olive said. "Whatever that means."

"Fashion inspiration from your grandmother may not be a good first look for the sixth grade," I said. We would have two-point-five seconds to make an impression on our fellow students and teachers at Featherstone Creek Middle School that would define how people saw us for the rest of our lives. At least that is what my dad told me about first impressions.

"Nia, what are you wearing?" Olive asked.

"Probably a skirt and my new denim jacket. Took me forever to get those rhinestones glued on, so you better believe I'm going to show off my work."

Man, why couldn't I design my own clothes, like Nia? What if I had the potential to be the next great American fashion designer like Vera Wang or Zac Posen and I'd never know it because my mom still picks out my clothes? All that potential, undiscovered. We were doing the world a disservice by not letting me pick out my own clothes!

"Girls! Food is almost ready!" my mom called from downstairs.

Nia and Olive moved toward the closet and quickly ruffled through my clothes. Nia found a white Vans T-shirt. "Pair this with that black denim skirt and you're set."

"Done," I said. "Statement made. Says 'sixth grade, here I am.'"

We gave each other high fives, then went downstairs and walked toward the back of the house for dinner.